The World

According to

Julia

A Murder Mystery

DEBORAH M. JONES is the author of works of theology and, apart from some drama for stage and radio, this is her first venture into fiction. She has a doctorate in the theology concerning the ethical treatment of animals and has worked as a copy-editor and newspaper editor, as well as a teacher and lecturer. She is passionate about both music and eighteenth-century literature, and lives a full life in Gloucestershire.

The World According to Julia

The World
According to Julia

Deborah M Jones

Rosehip Books

2015

The World According to Julia

Published in the UK by Rosehip Books – www.rosehipbooks.com

A portion of all proceeds from the sale of this book shall go to charity

First Published in Great Britain in 2015 by Rosehip Books.

ISBN 13: 978-1514226254

ISBN 10: 1514226251

Rosehip Books, UK

www.rosehipbooks.com

Chapter 1

THE ONLY FRAGMENT of my world worth telling you about is that which took place over the past few weeks. After all, murder doesn't happen very often. Not in my world.

My partner's? That's a different matter.

But we'll begin with me. My name is Julia, named after Julia Pendlebury, a girl in my mother's school whom she idolised. Young Pendlebury had been expelled for fomenting rebellion throughout the upper school. Mother's idea of a role model.

I am thirty-five, and totally non-rebellious. I'm also not bad looking, so my partner David assures me on the occasions when my confidence needs a boost (usually every four weeks or so). He could be a bit more lavish, but I'll settle for that.

My teenage years were spent in a male-free environment. At an all-girls grammar school, and more inclined to swot at weekends than to go clubbing, I rarely met boys. Besides, I actually enjoyed doing homework, at least by the time I got to the sixth form. Especially if it involved reading Jane Austen novels. However, the joy of learning was mixed with growing angst at never finding a boyfriend. By the time I went up to university, I was frantic. My fear was of missing out on the whole romantic love experience, but all that anxiety disappeared the moment I met David, my really wonderful partner (*Note to reader*, he's reading this…). I say 'partner' to sound trendy: actually he's my husband.

David is kind and loving, with even features and skin that tans well in the sun. Some women have even said they quite like being arrested by him. Enough, already.

When we met at university, David was studying law and then took a masters in criminology before entering the police service. Ever since watching episodes of Morse, it had been his childhood ambition to become a detective. Now he was.

Policing is that sort of no half-measures profession, a real vocation. You probably know all that from the many police-based TV programmes. According to these, your central police character will be a workaholic and probably an alcoholic, or otherwise have a dysfunctional and shambolic social life. Well, David certainly works with single-minded devotion (then, so do I) but in all other respects differs widely from his fictional counterparts.

David (he can't stand being called 'Dave') could not be shambolic in anything. He is incapable of messiness. My tendency to leave papers and books scattered around drives him crazy. It is my worst failing, according to him. (I don't want to know what the others are.) He is diligent and methodical, and wears neat, well-pressed clothes (which he irons himself, of course), with attention to clever colour co-ordination. Even his thick curly light-brown hair is tamed with the shortest cut above the shaven look.

He is, as he often says, devoted to two mistresses, his work and me. Well, that's fine. (So long as no number three ever comes along). I knew when I met him that a life in the police service would entail long unsocial hours and the prospect of annual leave being cut short at a moment's notice.

What I hadn't banked on was personal involvement in the crimes he was investigating.

Like this murder.

My work can be pretty obsession-inducing too. I teach Eng. Lit. at one of London's top universities, Queen's College. (I know what you're thinking – so why is my own writing style not more 'pure' and 'literary'? Well, I'm off-duty now. Professionally I write in the academic manner, stuffing the work with references and clever quotations.)

Like my departmental colleagues, I have a modern office on the sixth floor of the George Eliot building on Kingsway, near Aldwych and the Strand. Some of my fellow lecturers can be fun and good company, but there never seems time to socialise. Also, we all commute from distant parts of the capital and live miles away from each other, so meeting up after work does not often happen.

I say I teach. At least I try to do so. Actual contact time with students is increasingly squeezed out by administrative chores and paper- or computer-work. And, of course, by my own research. Anyone in academia knows the constant need to have written work published. Also we have to scrutinise erudite articles by other people in academic journals, fulfilling their peer-reviewed status. Then there are the books to review and edit, as well as simply to read to keep up with our subject. These days too we have to be familiar with all the relevant websites as they evolve in order to catch out students who crib from them. Plagiarising has never been so easy nor so hard to detect.

Of course there are lectures to prepare and on top of all that, we are expected to be available to meet the needs of each and every one of our students. Sounds like hard work? It is.

Yet there are moments – bright and beautiful ones – such as when I find one of my students enthusing over an eighteenth-century novel. Light shines in their eyes. The discovery that a book of 900-plus pages can be an actual joy to read!

Deep sigh from me.

It does not happen often. Most of my young female students, for the subject attracts mainly women, show big-eyed alarm when I ask them to tackle an assignment longer than a tweet. So, I tend to cultivate the interest of the keen ones and spend less energy on the others.

Nobody's perfect.

I still manage to push most of my students through graduation with reasonable degrees, and hope that, maybe, one day, they will return with something of fondness to the great classics of a bygone century.

Postgrads, on the other hand, are there because they love the subject. They are a delight. Also I am obliged to be pleasant and helpful to them. Some of them end up as colleagues, working alongside me.

I usually work in my office at college until the worst of the rush hour has passed, and then get the Northern Line or the number 11 bus to Chalk Farm and walk home from there.

David and I share a first floor apartment in a spacious (for London) early nineteenth-century townhouse in Camden, near where Karl Marx used to live, and close to the Dominican Priory where we both attend Mass.

David had been a leading light in the university Catholic Society when we met, and to please his family, I joined his Church before marrying him. I had started out attending the group meetings indifferently and simply out of love for him. Yet, when I was baptised in a grand Vigil service one Easter Saturday evening in David's home parish, I felt I had found a home. Here was a place from which I could journey further into the questions of meaning and belief for which religion has a language. Here too I could deepen my burgeoning relationship with God. The service, followed by a parish party that started near midnight and lasted into the early hours, was an event seared into my memory as one of life's great highlights.

So too was our wedding service, a Nuptial Mass, again in David's parents' parish church. Both ceremonies perfect in every way but one – my mother refused to attend either.

Let me tell you about her.

Mother, who insists on being called Helena (pronounced *Heleena*), never Mother or, worse, Mum, or Mummy, was not the person who brought me up. That was my grandmother Ivy who does not mind one jot being called Nana, Nana Ivy.

Nana is a formidable woman of great intelligence, now 86. She had been married for years to a quiet and devoted man who died in a work-related accident with a crane when I was very young. Having known poverty and hunger as a child in Liverpool, and deprived of much formal education, Nana Ivy sought knowledge and education not only as a means of escaping hardship but as an end in itself. She delights in whatever she learns about the world and its ways. It was she who instilled in me a love of books and language, and gently corrected my grammar and syntax as I spoke. She continued to do that even after I had graduated with a First in English and thought myself no end of an expert. As a widow, she has known the pain of loss. As a mother too.

It is only since I have grown up that I realise how her only daughter's estrangement must have hurt her. Helena rejected her family's aspirations as 'petty bourgeois', and opted for an Alternative Lifestyle, as we call it today. In those days it was called 'Dropping Out'. For Helena, all that mattered was to be 'real'. Worse even than being Middle Class was to be inauthentic. Her deepest contempt was for part-time hippies, students who posed as bohemian at college, only to resort to convention immediately upon graduation.

This is Helena's life, according to me. (It was a tendency of mine as a child to be unable to see the other person's point of view. Nana Ivy chided me with 'The world according to Julia' – a tag that became something of a catchphrase between us.)

Helena goes the whole way – with everything, except being a mother. Yes, she wanted a baby. She wanted one fathered by the alpha male of the commune. Tim was the supreme hippy, the one whom all the other women admired. She got her way. He obliged and I was born.

After a few years she passed me on to Nana Ivy, having balked at the prospect of enrolling me in the local Welsh-speaking primary school, some four miles away in that remote part of Conwy. Despite living in Wales, the national tongue was one of which none of the community could speak a word. Nor had she, nor any of the other women with whom she shared the rambling, shabby farm, the slightest intention of home-schooling me. All the children were farmed out to relatives.

Chapter 2

MY STORY BEGINS on Saturday morning, the first day of November, 2014. All Saints' Day, to be precise.

David had come in just after midnight, long after I had gone to bed to watch downloaded TV programmes on my ipad while I waited for him. It had been an unseasonably warm day and I had hoped we could go for a late evening walk up on Parliament Hill. It was not to be. Typical.

Anyway, I forgave him as he told me next day about the really important occurrence which had taken place. I could tell from the way David had spent the first part of the night tossing and kicking, ruffling up the bed linen and keeping me awake, that something was disturbing him. A little physical comforting from me in the early hours worked (for both of us), and he fell asleep until I woke him about seven with a cup of tea in bed.

As he took it he was somewhere else, somewhere which was excluding me. I demanded to know what was wrong.

'Murder', was all he said.

'So? Tell me about it?'

'Must I? It's too ....'

'No, go on. I'd sooner know than have you miserable all day.'

'You won't have me being miserable or anything else today. I'll have to go in. Sorry love. I've been put in charge. Senior Investigating Officer.'

'Wow, great! Not that you've got to go in on a day off. Nor that it's murder, of course, but...'

'Yeah, I know. It'll be good for me, but – it's just so sad. The victim is a girl, no more than eighteen or so. Obviously on her way to or from a Hallowe'en do...'

'How do you know that?'

'She was all in black. Head to toe. Like a million others out last night.'

'And how did she die?'

'Can't be sure; knifed, I think. Her face was all smashed in. Horrible. We'll know more after the PM.'

He looked ashen, the penalty of being sensitive. David was a rational, thinking man, but he could also feel deeply. It would not be beyond him to empathize keenly with what a victim must be suffering just before and at the moment of being killed. It gave him a driving commitment to bring justice to a victim. He could not bring back life, or undo injury, but he could bring the perpetrator to confront what he or she had done. And maybe bring about a transformation of character. Redemption, or retribution. Either way.

He had been a detective inspector with the Met, based at Paddington Green Police Station, for eighteenth months. In that time he had been responsible for investigating several sudden deaths. This is London, after all. But a mysterious murder of a young woman is the kind of high-profile investigation that could make or break a career.

He was adept at solving gang-land murders, or domestic quarrels that had accelerated into fatal batterings. Murder upsets the right order of things, but some of them are fairly straightforward: most people who kill have neither the time nor intelligence to cover their traces. They tend to be caught fairly quickly and brought to justice in the fullness of time.

But this was different. It could have been a stranger crime, perhaps by a lunatic. Whatever, this one seemed to have questions marks all over it. The negative aspect for the investigating team would be the long hours, nervous exhaustion, frustration and endless waiting. But who knows? The crime might be solved within days, and laurels rightfully bestowed.

'I suppose you'll be working all tomorrow too. That means I'll have to go to Mass alone – again.' Wrinkled nose of disappointment.

I finished my tea and once more heaved myself out of bed. I performed the necessary ablutions and slopped along to the kitchen in matching white toweling mules and bath robe.

By the time David appeared, having washed, dressed and shaved, I had made the toast and was pouring coffee. He had some time before leaving, so, after munching a round of marmaladed toast, he took out the file of papers relating to the case, avoiding odd sticky splodges on the table.

Some A4-sized photographs caught my eye.

'Can I see?'

'I'd rather you didn't...'

Too late. I snatched one and studied it. A body lying on the ground, dark. Dark clothes, dark ground, dark unrecognisable face. Or rather, a bloody mess that did not even look much like a face. I did not want to examine that too closely.

'Hey, give it back.'

No laughter from him. Not the time or subject for a playful tug of war or teasingly holding it at arm's length. I returned it and peered over his shoulder at it and the other gruesome images he was holding, before turning to clear the breakfast remains. I wiped the table so that he could spread out the dozen or so photographs.

He stared at one, a close-up of the upper legs of the victim.

'What do you think those are?'

He pointed to one of the thighs, where there were traces of two or three short, almost horizontal, stripes made by something like chalk. They marked the front of her left leg, and at the lowest would have been roughly an inch above the knee. I had seen those sorts of marks before, but could not remember where.

'Was her face painted, or anything else Hallowe'eny about her?'

'Can't tell. The face.... (*deep sigh*)... But the black clothes...they, y'know, seeing as half of London was all in black last night. Honestly, some of them, young kids, wandering round the streets in skeleton costumes or as witches, or had mock blood all over them. Stupid! Where were the parents?'

The girl was too old for trick or treating, that odious American import. Probably just partying or clubbing. Maybe she had a mask somewhere? Not found.

'When was she found?'

'About nine last night. Been dead an hour or so. The scene-of-crime team couldn't be sure. They're probably still there.

Bit early for clubbing. Maybe a private party/

Poor girl. The same age as most of my students. She could have been one of them.

'Where was she found?'

Not near my college, please, oh please.

'Near here. The other side of Hampstead Heath, almost hidden by bushes. Propped up against a tree-trunk. She was found by a couple of blokes. They'd gone over to this copse, apparently, for a little, um, cuddle, when they almost fell over her. They were really, really upset. Put them off their night of passion. One threw up nearby when he saw the face, or what was left of it.'

Smashing a face meant it would take time to identify the victim. Presumably that was the point. Or sheer hatred. If too badly disfigured, it would not be possible to reconstruct her face, which the police would need to do for distributing photographs. It might even be impossible to track the dental records. The killer would know that the longer it took, the less likely he or she could be found. The first few hours and days are vital to any investigation. As is finding the murder weapon.

'Any sign of the weapon?'

'None.'

'You don't suspect either or both of the gay guys, do you? Isn't it often the person who "finds" the body, the one who did it?'

'Possibly. But unlikely in this case. You can just tell. I can go back to them if I need more info, but they come across as genuine enough. One is a retired accountant, the other works in a shoe shop. Anyway, must go. A lot to do, especially as forensics won't be producing anything until Monday; they've such a backlog. At least they're working over the weekend.

He stood up and gathered the photographs together, slipping them into his briefcase.

'Meanwhile,' he sighed, 'I wish I knew what those marks are on her thigh.'

We kissed, he left, and I got dressed. I cleared up a little and washed the crockery, listening to the radio while I pottered about usefully. Then I put on my coat and went out on foot to the food shops on Haverstock Hill to replenish supplies.

Coming back into the welcome warmth of the flat, I made for myself a cheese sandwich and a coffee, and settled down to read and mark some student essays; a dozen versions of why Richardson's hefty tome *Clarissa* was or was not the greatest book in the language. It was certainly the longest, as were these essays. After napping involuntarily, I remembered to telephone Nana Ivy as I always tried to do on a Saturday, and then I went through more tedious papers.

That's unfair. They were not all bad. Some showed that the writers had, at least, read the book involved.

It was dark long before David returned and we shared a ready meal from *Marks & Spencer*, microwaved with professional expertise. A bottle of Chilean red wine helped soothe away the day's cares, and we slumped in front of *Strictly Come Dancing* and then a film before heading for bed.

Then it hit me. Out of the blue, as I was getting between the sheets. Of course. I knew what those marks mean! Do I tell him now, and set him off on a trail that might last all night? Or wait until morning? I decided it was only fair to wait. After all, I might have had my brainwave during the night rather than getting in to bed. I'd sleep on it and see if I still thought it made sense the next day.

Next morning I woke my sleepy-eyed partner by bringing him a Sunday morning coffee in bed. I was usually the one served on a Sunday, but this morning I was bursting with my idea. He smiled, propped himself up on the pillows and asked me to tell him what it was to cause such a break from routine.

'Well, you know those marks on the trouser leg? I remember where I have seen similar before. They are, I think, the marks of the rosin from the bow of a cello. When you play the highest string, the one on the far left, the tip of the bow sometimes accidentally slightly scrapes across your thigh, leaving traces of the rosin.'

'What is this rosin thing?'

'It's a lump of hard resin, extracted mainly from pine trees. It comes in, like, a small round cake. You rub it up and down the hairs of the bow.'

'What for?'

'It helps the hairs, the horsehairs, to grip the strings, to get them to vibrate and make the sound. Otherwise your bow might just slip around. I remember using it – it looks a bit like amber – when I learned to play the cello years ago. Nana Ivy paid for a few lessons. I stopped because I was never going to be a concert cellist and couldn't be bothered practising every day.

But what I've noticed, going to concerts, is that some cellists mark themselves more than others. Particularly people playing the baroque cello – that's one you have to grip between your knees. That type've got no pin, the stick-thingy that normal cellos have, to hold it up from the floor. So you have to hold it in place by pressing it between your knees, like riding a horse. Anyway, the baroque cello is held closer to the body, so it makes it more likely that the player will touch the left leg as he or she plays, especially when they play down by the bridge. Got it?'

'So you're saying our victim was a baroque cello player?'

'Yes, possibly – and that's why she was in black! She was dressed in performance clothes.'

'I thought all musicians wore sexy evening dresses. You know – low cut and glittery.'

'That's only the stars, the soloists. The orchestral players keep to black, trousers or whatever.'

'So, according to you – and I'm not saying you're wrong – our girl is a baroque cellist on her way to play in a concert?'

'On her way from, yes, hence the marks already – although if she was killed about eight o'clock, that rather rules out ...'

My voice tailed off as I could not imagine a concert having finished by eight.

Then, another bolt.

'Ah! I've got it! You know the Royal College of Music has those drive-time concerts, or whatever they're called...early evening things. They start at six and go on for an hour. I know because I was introduced to them by a Royal College student, you know, Toyah, that nice black post-grad who comes to me for occasional tutorials?'

'And the Royal College – that's the one behind the Albert Hall, not the one in Marylebone Street?'

'Yes! That other one is the Royal Academy. Big rival. They have early evening recitals too, I think.'

'My lovely, clever girl!'

David's face lit up and he lunged at me suddenly, embracing me with real warmth and affection. Help – the coffee mug! No problem. On the bedside table. How could I doubt David's forethought.

He went off to his police station, buoyed by this not unreasonable line of enquiry, while I got myself ready and went early to the eleven o'clock Mass, in time to light a candle and pray for the young victim and her family.

Chapter 3

Sunday evening.

DAVID RETURNED LATE, but by then he knew the identity of the victim. Fingerprints confirmed that she was, indeed, a student at the Royal College of Music and had been playing there in a recital of Scarlatti string quartet music early on Friday evening.

The other three members of the group, when they were tracked down, knew only that she, Sophie Anderson, had received a text on her mobile phone as she was packing up her instrument, and that she had left the building at about seven o'clock without saying anything, apart from the normal farewell and a check on the time of the next rehearsal.

That was not unusual.

Sophie, it seems, was a rather private person from a moneyed background who had a few close friends but was not gregarious. She never socialised beyond her own group, and seemed rather contemptuous of her contemporaries. Her fellow quartet players were not among these close friends, although they all got on reasonably well together. Sophie was something of a star player, very intense and ambitious. Poor girl.

She had been wearing a quilted navy anorak, a white woollen scarf and carrying her cello when she left the building. This particular cello was an instrument of great value, and was carried in a black fibreglass case. None of these items, nor her mobile phone, was on or near her when she was found. Her phone must have been disabled, as it could not be traced. The CCTV camera in the front of the building could have picked up on her getting into a vehicle, but was not working and had been out of action for a few days. No other street camera showed anything of interest.

According to David, the College Director had been really helpful, specially returning from his weekend break with friends in the Surrey countryside. He had provided lists of students, staff and the dozen or so ticket holders who had ordered their free tickets for the Friday concert on-line or by telephone.

David's team had all the following-up to do – there could be weeks of work for them, even with all the resources available for the Met by the Homicide and Serious Crime Command (HASCC), its Homicide Task Force (HTF) and the advanced computer system, known by its witty acronym HOLMES (Home Office Large Major Enquiry Service). Despite all the technology and trained personnel, nothing replaced the sheer slog of questioning people. The team engaged in interviewing as many names on the lists as they could in the hope of building up a sufficient body of information to make intelligent guess work, which is what so much of crime investigation entails.

Some of the late Miss Anderson's fellow students were interviewed during the day, but Sunday was not a good time for meeting members of the public face to face. Most of those who had been to the recital were at home when telephoned or emailed but nearly all lived at some distance from the college, even in one case as far away as South Wales. They may have to be available to be called in during the week, if necessary. They all expressed shock and sorrow at the loss of such a talented young performer to whose playing it had been a pleasure to listen.

An interview room had been arranged in the College, and the Director was compliance itself. He was upset, as were the members of staff, at the brutal loss of one of their young undergraduates.

The worst job in the police service is giving to the stricken parents the news of such a death. This ordeal had not yet been accomplished by the time David returned home. There had been no response at the Anderson's main residence, a grand country mansion in Norfolk, when the local police had called round.

The Director recalled that the girl's father was not on the scene, and furnished the police with addresses of secondary, or holiday, homes for the mother, one in France and one in Barbados. She could have been at either of these, although bets were on that she would spend the winter months in Barbados and the summer ones in France. She would have to be tracked down on Monday.

I took David's mind off his all-absorbing problem in the usual wifely way. It worked, and we both slept well.

Chapter 4

ON MONDAY I WENT to Queen's and David to the music college to start with his allocation of interviews. I spent part of the morning at a departmental planning meeting making tedious arrangements for the second semester, with its preceding examinations. Then I took a seminar. The students were on good form after the weekend, and their brightness and ready laughter gave me a brief respite from the gloomy thoughts of murder.

In the afternoon I was scheduled to have another meeting with Toyah Lane, the doctoral student at the Royal College of Music who had asked me to help with her research. As I was not her official supervisor of studies, being employed by a different institution from hers, my reward was to have her initiate me into the London concert scene.

Although I had been living in London for ten years, I had not been to a recital at the Wigmore Hall. Toyah recommended one by an eminent quartet. I loved every minute. Since then I have become one of their regulars, and haunt other such places. I go by myself as David is more of a popular music fan, although we occasionally treat ourselves to a night at a musical or opera.

Toyah has been seeing me for over a year with the blessing of her own supervisor. Her thesis involves researching the sources and influences of the composer and music historian, Dr Charles Burney, 1746-1814. He was the father of the novelist, letter-writer and journal-keeper, Frances (known as Fanny) Burney, who is my own special subject of teaching and research.

I know something of the Burney family, although there are fellow members of the Burney Society who can always outshine me with their grasp of the most recherché of facts. The Burney's was such a prodigiously talented and lively family that there is always more to find out about their lives and writings. I love talking with postgrads who share my enthusiasm for them, and Toyah's was almost as great as my own. She knew more about the musical side of the self-made patriarch Charles, whereas I could fill in something of his literary circle and general social background.

Although we were due to meet at two, her not showing up enabled me to catch up on paperwork, such as more essay marking and beginning to fine-tune the next day's lecture notes. By three, I decided to call her.

A tearful voice replied.

Of course.

I had not made the connection that this twenty-four-year-old could well know a young undergraduate at the same college. In fact, had she not mentioned a 'Sophie' as one of her friends? We had not really discussed much about Toyah's social life as when we met there was always so much to say about the Burney family and about music in general.

I then caught another couple of words although my thoughts had obscured most of them. 'Police' and 'interview'. Ah, David and Toyah, coming together, although it could be someone else on his team who would interview her.

We rescheduled our meeting for the following day, when I had a couple of hours between the lecture, a seminar and two more meetings. My head of department needed to see me about something and I had to see the university librarian about stocking some particular titles that would be useful next term. That always led to a prolonged session of haggling that would be familiar to traders in an oriental bazaar. I always included a few extra titles that I didn't really want and that I would deliberately drop from my 'wish-list', thus showing my reasonableness and general affability. Cunning, huh? It always pays to keep librarians on-side.

Shortly after three o'clock, I began a series of interviews with individual students wanting either help with assignments or permission to avoid doing them altogether. One young man wanted to drop out of the course he had been on for barely six weeks. Better now than later, I suppose. But I disliked his expectation of a degree with no preliminary work. Anyhow, I got away just after the rush hour and returned home to find a note under the door.

My mother, my rarely-seen commune-dweller, had arrived to stay and, finding me out (Of course! What did she expect on a weekday in term time?), was being given shelter by the elderly, ultra-respectable gentleman, Mr Hobson, who lives in the flat below ours. I felt the anger rising in me. Why on earth had she not telephoned or warned me somehow of her arrival? Who said she could just turn up? What made her think she'd be welcome here? And how dare she impose upon the gentle, amiable old duffer who just happened to be a neighbour.

I dumped my briefcase, shoulderbag and coat and tore downstairs, breathing fire. Mr Hobson's smiling face on opening the door to my loud knocking rather quenched the flames.

'You've come for your mother.' Stating the obvious. 'Come in, come in! We were just having the most amusing time. Your mother has a wealth of interesting stories. You must let her come to see me again. Would you like a cup of something, or a sherry?'

My mother stood up smiling broadly.

'Ronald and I were telling each other tales of our youth,' she said, taking his hand as if they were old and close friends.

Ronald! I dreaded the nature of their conversation. It was unlikely that 'Ronald' had had a chance to say anything at all, but was no doubt benumbed and beguiled by accounts alien to anything he had known. Drug-fuelled parties, sex on tap and accounts of midnight skinny-dipping in strangers' pools. The list could be endless. None of it uplifting.

I was mortified to be associated with this shameless woman, this mother of mine. I forced my face into a charming smile for Mr Hobson's sake, prized my mother's hand from her victim's, and led her, rather forcefully, away. Just as she made the foot of the stairs, she remembered her luggage – a bulging sturdy plastic bag in candy pink and white stripes, which I went back into Mr Hobson's hallway to retrieve, and obliged her to precede me up the stairs.

I had calmed down considerably by the time we got into the flat and I saw the pathetic amount of what passed for my mother's luggage – her entire wardrobe: a pair of shabby jeans and some long skirts of earth-tones enhanced by a patina of unshiftable dirt. Some loose woollen tops vaguely complemented the outfits and a couple of floaty garments,

presumably kaftans, in Indian cotton betokening warmer
weather. She was wearing her only coat, a padded jacket with
pockets torn from having had large items stuffed into them.

'What brings you here, Mother? Sorry, Helena...
Why on earth could you not have warned me?'

'Well, Petal, if that's your attitude, I'll go. I'll not
stop where I'm not wanted.'

'I'm sorry. I didn't mean that. It's not that I don't
want to see you, but it would be nice to have some warning.
Why, and why now? And what's with this "Petal" business?
It's a long way from "Comrade" or, what was it last time?
"Thingy" – because you couldn't remember my name!'

'Now then, don't be bitchy. It doesn't suit you. Well,
we've got a couple of new people who've joined us, and one is
Ann, a lovely woman about my age, from South Wales,
Merthyr, and everyone is Petal or Flower to her. I've just
caught it, is all.'

She always was impressionable, picking up the
accent of whoever she was speaking with, and now talks with
a slight Welsh lilt.

'Anyway, the generator packed in, the diesel one –
well, to tell you the truth, we can't afford the diesel right now.
The other one, the tractor-driven one, isn't so good, and the
place is bloody freezing. So I thought of you in this snug little
flat and knew you could give me a bed. Well, somewhere to
sleep, over the coldest of the winter.'

Worse than I feared. Not a flying visit, then.

Helena's arrival was not warmly welcomed by David either. He did his best to appear moderately, politely, delighted, but I could tell he found the situation fell short of perfection. He found my mother difficult to cope with and her casual use of recreational drugs was deeply embarrassing to him. We both hoped she had brought none with her. We had wanted to discuss the murder case, but waited until we turned in for an 'early night', leaving my mother watching television on the sofa which we had made up into her bed.

'We wouldn't give houseroom to one of these TVs,' she called out, loftily. Yet she sat entranced watching any rubbishy programme until the early hours. Her habit was to leave the appliance on while she slept until David or I, not standing the canned laughter coming from the sitting room, would sneak in to turn it off.

When we were alone together, he brought me up to speed on the enquiry.

No wonder the mother could not be found in Norfolk. The local police in Barbados had located her in the Queen Elizabeth Hospital, Bridgetown, to which she had been taken after a heart attack not long after arriving to spend the winter months. Her male partner, younger and, from his photograph, very good looking in a Sean-Connery way, had flown back to England to 'settle some affairs', he had told the doctors. He was seeing solicitors, bankers and others, in the likely event of Mrs Anderson never fully recovering. She could not be told of her daughter's death now as, even if she could hear and understand, the delicacy of her heart would not take such a shock. The partner was being traced and would be interviewed as soon as he was found.

David and I looked at each other in silence for a moment. Then one of us muttered that phrase that Cicero used so tellingly, 'Cui bono?' And the other nodded, knowingly. Who benefits from the heiress's death?

'He's obviously a suspect. I'll interview him myself. I did see Sophie's boyfriend today. Surly lad. That public school arrogance about him. He is not a musician, but doing some kind of computer stuff at Imperial.

'Right next door.' The two colleges were neighbours.

'Yes. Hey, I also spoke to a young woman, mixed race, very attractive, who's doing research in your area, that Burney bloke!'

'Toyah Lane. Yes, I told you about her. She should have come to me this afternoon for one of our chats about Dr Burney. I rang her and she mentioned something about the police and interviews. It must have been about three o'clock.'

'Ah, I'd been chatting to her while she was waiting for Frances, you know, Sergeant White, to interview her. Helpful girl, your Toyah. She shared a house with Sophie. But she was very upset, very weepy. When are you seeing her next?'

'Tomorrow.'

'Well, see what you can get out of her that might be useful. You can sometimes think of the sort of thing that others can't. And I don't reckon much on Frances White having a razor sharp mind! She's OK. Steady and reliable, but a bit lacking in imagination.'

We then got on to the subject of my mother, and for how long she would be staying. We contemplated escaping somewhere and leaving her in the flat. It wouldn't work, but was a diverting thought. If only it had been Nana Ivy instead of mother. She would be unobtrusive and make herself useful, washing up while I worked quietly on papers and books, and letting David have his choice of TV programmes when he got in at night.

Instead we were in for a few weeks or months of endless complaints about our collusion with capitalism and the way we were destroying the atmosphere, let alone corrupting the minds of the young with useless learning.

She would, on past evidence, harangue us for upholding laws which had been passed by politicians who 'were all corrupt and self-seeking'. All, without exception. Fault would be found with the food we prepared, even while she consumed it in prodigious quantities.

We failed to see eye to eye on the subject of meat. She ate it, and we do not. She detests all processed food, calling it 'unnatural'. Animal products from farms which raise animals intensively she would denounce as 'evil'. And yet she could happily wring the neck, pluck and eat one of the chickens scratching around the farm yard of their commune, or take one of their sheep to slaughter and butcher the carcass. Dead animals in themselves are not the problem for her.

My vegetarianism, begun under Nana Ivy's influence when I was small, was based on the sympathy felt with any animal having its life terminated for my sake. Now that I realize the way Western livestock production takes resources from the developing world seals my commitment. Poor David, who has no such qualms about what he eats when away from home, obligingly abjures all meat when with me, although I even offer to cook it for him. His amenable nature is one of the reasons I love him so much.

Chapter 5

Tuesday morning

THE NEXT MORNING he and I skipped breakfast and left the flat before Helena stirred, and I wondered with what information Toyah would be able to provide me that she had not already told to the police. I could not do police work, or be seen to be interfering, but could maybe pick up something here and there that might help to build up a picture of Sophie's, the victim's, life and last movements.

When the young postgraduate turned up at the appointed time she was certainly lacking her usual sparkle. A caring and kindly girl, she had been offered counseling, but thought that doing some work would be better in helping to heal the grief.

We talked for some time about Burney and his impression of music on his European tours, but it was hard to concentrate on an eighteenth-century figure when the present time impinged so radically.

She let me ask her some questions, first about herself and then about Sophie, and how long they had known each other.

It transpired that Toyah had been born to a black hotel manageress in Barbados. A career woman, she had no time to raise a child. So Toyah, christened Toyah-Jane but dropping the 'Jane', had been brought up in the home of her white father, a bass-player in the hotel's band, whose childless wife had loved her as her own. They were not well off, and suffered further when the father was obliged to support two further children born to Barbadian women.

Then, in her teens, as a talented young musician showing great promise, Toyah had won scholarships, first to a specialist music school in the West of England, and then to the Royal College of Music.

As for many years Sophie's mother had wintered near her own home in Barbados, Toyah and Sophie had met together at occasional social and musical functions during the Christmas holidays. Despite the disparity of age, Toyah at twenty-four being four years older than Sophie, their shared interest in music enabled them to enjoy each other's company. If anything, Toyah said that she often felt the younger of the two. Sophie, for all her faults, and I was beginning to learn what some of them were, was neither a snob nor a racist.

Toyah was a fine harpsichord player, and she and the young cellist had performed a few times together on the island and practised in each other's home.

When Sophie was accepted at the Royal College, she had wanted to rent a house, rather than stay in a hall of residence. Toyah had spent her undergrad years in university accommodation and was glad for the chance to be more independent. So Sophie, Toyah, and another young musician, Rachel Finklemann, took a house in Fulham that would have been beyond the pocket of most students. Sophie's mother footed two-thirds of the bill, with Toyah and Rachel paying the difference between them.

Even that was a lot for Toyah, with relatively limited funds and facing eventual repayment of her student debt, even with a scholarship. She made some money giving flute and harpsichord lessons, and was entrusted with a small amount of teaching and accompanying at the Royal College of Music.

Then I asked her more about Sophie, what she was really like.

'Oh, she was beautiful!' Toyah said generously. 'But she could be moody. She could turn on smiles and charm and then, pow! switch to blasting someone for something really trivial.'

'Did she blast at you?'

'Not really, nor Rachel. I think she was a bit in awe of Rachel. Rachel's so...controlled. To us she was a loyal friend. To everyone, so long as she got what she wanted, she was really a pleasant person. She practised a lot, really dedicated. I think she wanted to be rich and famous in her own right, apart from her mother's wealth. Most of her free time, when she was not practising, was spent with Matt, that's her boyfriend. Actually she also went out with some older men. She let them escort her to dinner or the theatre.'

Older men? My eyes opened wide.

'Well, that's Sophie. She knew that her looks could make people want to do things for her, and, like, she exploited that for all she was worth.'

I must have looked a little shocked.

'Oh, she saw no harm in it and believed that it was...'

'A fair exchange for bestowing her smiles and attention!' I added, smiling to hide my disapproval. 'What did, whatsisname, Matt make of that?'

'He did not seem to mind. I think he knew that he couldn't afford to keep Sophie..'

'In the style of life to which she was accustomed?'

'Yeah, that's it. He knows, knew, that she always returns to him. They'd laugh about these old guys, her admirers. Here, I've got some photos. Not of them, but of Sophie.'

She took out her smartphone from her jeans pocket and clicked through to find the photographs she wanted, then passed it over to me to look at them.

I saw Toyah smiling with another girl in a couple of selfies. The other, obviously Sophie, was attractive, even beautiful, and obviously took good care of her appearance. Her figure was fuller than currently fashionable; voluptuous, rather than plump. She had an oval face, with baby-smooth complexion, large green eyes which were wide apart and thickly lashed, and full, sculptured lips. To destroy such a face as that with brutal force must have been the result of overwhelming hatred.

'Like I said: you know what she did?' Toyah smiled mischievously. 'When she was out with these older guys, she would stop in front of a shop window to admire a piece of jewellery, or a bottle of designer perfume, something really, really expensive. She'd do that thing with her eyes. Go all appealing, like, so the bloke would feel obliged to buy it and give it to her as a gift.'

'The little minx!' I tried to say it non-judgmentally, but without much success. I am such a prude.

I asked who her latest escorts had been, and was told that one of them was a famous, though happily married, musician, a pianist performing in all the world's major musical venues. Sophie had never let on who it was, and Toyah had decided it would be safer not to ask. He never came to the house, and Sophie would arrange to meet him in whichever hotel he was staying in.

The most recent of her 'beaux' had been one of the most generous to her. Clothes, perfume, theatre. None of it cheap. He was a visiting American scholar working at the Royal College, something of a celebrity in the music-history world. He had recently made the musical discovery of the century: an extensive sketch of a piece of music by Haydn, with several pages of actual composition, that was not previously known to exist. It formed the first draft of another oratorio to match and complete *The Creation*, as the subject concerned the Last Judgement. The manuscript, with an accompanying letter, had been addressed to Dr Charles Burney, Haydn's English contact and agent. It was Burney who had encouraged Haydn to write oratorios for the London market in the tradition of the earlier Handel.

The newly discovered Haydn piece and the letter were dated 1802, the final year of Haydn's musical production before debilitating illness. They were found together in the library of a private schloss in Austria, and had been enclosed in a folder and sealed, but had never, for some reason, been sent.

Toyah's interest in Dr Charles Burney was the link between this eminent academic and her house mate, Sophie. Toyah had arranged for a tutorial with Dr Oakwood on the subject. To her disappointment, it had not yet taken place. He had promised to see her when he had a free moment as he was engaged for much of his time in teaching early keyboard music to undergraduates. So Toyah had invited him to her house to appraise and play her harpsichord. She hoped then to discuss her research project with him, but just before she could, Sophie had appeared and totally bewitched him.

As Toyah put it, Sophie had 'got off with him' and she was left in the background. That was Sophie all over.

I asked about Rachel. How was she taking the tragedy? Toyah had not seen her since the weekend, as Rachel had gone home to Leeds and not returned. That was quite normal, apparently. Rachel often went home as her parents demanded her company at certain home entertainments of theirs, for which she was expected to play the violin and piano. She would stay on for a few days and return when all her family commitments were accomplished.

Also Rachel had a boyfriend in Leeds and they could not bear to be parted. Toyah had texted her about Sophie, but she had so far not replied.

Chapter 6

THAT EVENING, HELENA was out, leaving a note to say she woul be back 'sometime'. David updated me on his investigation and I told him of my time with Toyah.

He was intrigued by the details of the two older, distinguished men with whom Sophie had associated within the past few months. Apparently, and sadly predictably, Sergeant Frances White had not extracted that information during her interview with Toyah. Instead she had concentrated on how the three young women all got on together in the house and what Toyah had thought of Sophie's boyfriend. What particularly interested the sergeant were the relationships between Sophie, her mother and the mother's new partner. Amicable, apparently.

David's team had turned up an interesting expansion of the fact that Sophie's instrument, an old Italian baroque cello, was such an expensive one. Her mother had bought it for her the previous May at a Bonhams auction sale in London for a six-figure sum. Even the bow she bought to go with it cost her over £5,000. I knew they could be expensive but that is amazing.

I wondered how anyone could entrust a student with an instrument of such expense. I did not begrudge people their wealth. My envy was attached solely to those whose lives of ease could give them time to read widely and deeply. Lack of time was my poverty, always was.

Mrs Anderson had given this über-cello to Sophie for her 20th birthday in July and the girl had reserved its use for concerts and recitals. Another, less costly, cello was the one she brought to and from the college, or stashed it in a locker, and used for normal practising and rehearsals.

The other quartet members had not seen the new instrument before Friday's concert. They had been impressed by its tone and hoped it had not outshone their own playing too much.

The fact that the costly cello and bow were not with the body may have been significant.

David's eyes narrowed with intensity as he mentioned his next discovery.

One of the disappointed bidders at the auction of top-end musical intruments had been commissioned to purchase it for a Russian oligarch whose own daughter was learning to play the baroque cello. This Russian father, on a business trip to London, had approached Sophie as she was entering college one morning. He had asked her, rather forcefully, if she would be willing to sell it to him for the price it went for, plus £10,000. He would collect it himself as he knew where she lived.

Sophie refused, but this last comment, spoken almost under his breath, had alarmed her considerably. She reported the incident to her tutor straight away.

The poor woman was distraught, so David reported, blaming herself for having reassured the girl and not suggesting she reported it to the police.

My fears that possible Russian involvement in this murder could be the cause of an unpleasant international incident, with Foreign Office interference and political pressures. This Russian had obviously gone to some trouble to find the possessor of the instrument. Who knows if he would have gone further?

'Don't worry,' was David's response. 'If he's our man, we'll get him. It shouldn't be too hard to track him down from Bonham's files.'

'And if he's gone back to Russia? What if he's a friend of the President?'

'That could be a bit of a drawback, but he must be questioned. Maybe I'll have to go to Moscow or somewhere for a bit.' He grinned. David was never averse to a foreign trip, especially now with Helena living in our apartment. Extradition, he conceded, might be difficult. He would have to check on that.

One thing that could help if the cello were ever to come up for sale in a shop or at auction anywhere in the world were the high definition photographs and other details taken by Bonhams of their prestigious sale items.

David went on to mutter his oft-spoken mantra, that what would really help people to be reunited with their stolen belongings would be if they applied Smartwater to their precious goods. That was one of his hobby-horses, and I made a mental note to acquire some of the magic potion for our few bits of semi-valuables. That we did not already have any ourselves was among the things I just did not feel like sharing.

David was quite hopeful that, if this were a simple theft of valuable property 'gone wrong' (though what constitutes going 'right'?) it could be quite a straightforward crime to solve. Find the instrument, do all the fingerprint and DNA checks, and Bob's your uncle. If only life were that simple.

Unfortunately, the forensic department had nothing positive to report from the scene of the crime. No hairs of anyone other than the victim's, or flakes of skin, or traces of fabric were found on the body. Maybe the coat was covered in them, but that was not there. The killer knew how to cover his or her tracks. (I could not imagine it being a 'her', but you never know.) It takes a cool head to realize that evidence would be on the bloodied coat and to carefully remove it, by gloved hands, after the killing.

The postmortem revealed that there had been a knife wound to the chest, followed by strangulation and then heavy blows to the face, no doubt to delay recognition of the victim and so give the killer longer time in which to dispose of evidence and maybe get far away. As far as Russia? Time alone would tell, if at all.

Tomorrow would produce more interviews, and more checks on alibis. A breakthrough, if there was to be one, could happen at any time – soon, or much, much later.

We both caught ourselves sighing together, thinking of the long and tedious hours ahead for the investigation team – tracking people down and talking to them, checking their statements, working out logistics, reading realms of paperwork and occasionally someone having a brainwave that might, just, lead somewhere.

David had spent some time at the crime scene, trying to discern a way in which two people – with or without a sizeable instrument case – could walk across Hampstead Heath, in the dark, then one kill the other over a few minutes, and yet nobody saw anything. One or two routes across the Heath avoided all CCTV cameras, and as nothing suggestive of the forms of victim and killer appeared on the tapes, the killer must have reccied the route beforehand. This implied careful forethought, not an impulse killing.

Had there been a shouting match? Had she screamed? Was she taken along the paths or dragged over the grass by force, struggling, or threatened at knifepoint? Or did she walk willingly, unsuspectingly, alongside her killer, talking, even laughing – until she suspected?

There were no signs of a struggle anywhere other than where the body was found, and no sign of a murder weapon. An easily-hidden long-bladed knife was the primary weapon, but something hard, harder than fists, had smashed her cheekbones, nose and jaw.

Someone had gone to the meeting prepared to do violence. The sheer force and intensity used seemed to rule out another woman, or even a slight man, unless he was really fit.

These morbid musings of the copper and his missus were eventually relieved by the return home of my wayward mother.

Helena actually provided a cheerful antidote, beaming at us as she did. I did not ask her where she had been, and she did not volunteer it. I did remember to thank her for having left a note – surprisingly thoughtful for her. I put together a light supper for us all, and later even made us all hot chocolate, comfort food.

Helena turned on the television and we left her watching a satirical comedy. We could hear the studio audience loving it, whooping and laughing at every facile joke. I might have done so too, after a few drinks and on another evening.

Chapter 7

Wednesday, Guy Fawkes Day

THIS WAS A DAY I HAD been looking forward to for a while. I left Helena a ten pound note and a Post-it, asking her to get in some groceries. David left early, as I did.

I reached college an hour before the usual time, getting a coffee and croissant on the way. I spent the first hour doing some initial preparation for a talk I was to give in a couple of weeks time at the Chawton House Library in Hampshire.

Then I saw Tom Jacobs for an hour, a doctoral student having difficulties finding original material for his thesis.

After that I joined colleagues from the Theatre and Performance Studies section of the English Department. We met in the Greenwood Theatre, south of the river near Guy's Hospital. We were to begin auditioning for a pair of plays by

Fanny Burney which we planned to produce during the following semester. We had chosen *The Witlings* and *Love and Fashion*. I had pushed hard for these to be performed, knowing that a production could both stimulate a new interest in the author, and also give the undergrads a sense of her radical nature and even early feminist leanings.

Auditions were going reasonably well although some students simply recited their learned short sections of one of the plays in a mechanical, tuneless way. Others assumed that live theatre was like television, where mumbling is *de rigeur*. Just as the most promising young woman, of expressive voice and lively manner, was launching in to her role, the mobile phone went off in my bag. Crescendoing pling-plong-plingety plong – plingy, plongy, pling....

Embarrassed and flustered, I took the call. It was from Toyah, and hearing her verge-of-tears tone, I went out of the room to continue the call.

'Sorry to bother you, Julia,' she almost sobbed. 'But I can't face it. I just can't. Not now.'

'Face what? And calm down, Toyah. What's the matter, apart from the obvious?'

'I've got to play tonight. I'm accompanying my friend, a singer at the Academy, and I just can't face it. I can't practise at home, not without Sophie there. Knowing.... And what will I do with the house? I'll have to find somewhere else, and I've got no money, none to speak of...'

'Hold on, there. What time is your concert? Seven-thirty? You're at home? OK! I'll be there in an hour. Do something else for a time. Have something to eat and look up those references I suggested. See you.'

I made my excuses and left, as journalists say. A tube journey and short walk later and I was strolling up the path to the front door of a smart terraced villa in Fulham.

Part of the house, Sophie's bedroom, and the shared sitting room, was cordoned off with yellow and black police marker tape, as the forensic team wanted them to be unpolluted should they need to return for further investigations.

Toyah met me at the door and took me along the hallway, passing the taped-off doorway to the sitting room, and on into the room behind it – a former dining-, turned into a music-room.

Book cases held scores and programmes as well as standard books, and there was Toyah's harpsichord, taking centre stage, with instruments and their cases around the room. There was a large recorder, which Toyah told me was a tenor one, Sophie's second instrument for college, although she was also doing singing studies. I asked about Sophie's regular cello and was told that she had left that in a locker at college as she would have used it for practising there. She rarely practised at home. Toyah pointed to a flute in disassembled pieces in an open case. That was her second instrument; and a violin and an oboe which belonged to Rachel. That third housemate had returned earlier that morning and was out buying items of food for the next few days.

We continued into the kitchen, where Toyah took down a jar of instant coffee and made a couple of mugs of the tasteless brown liquid. We sat at the kitchen table and she thanked me for turning up.

'My problem,' she almost sobbed, 'is the loss. There's a gap in the house. Sophie's voice; her presence. Even when we didn't get on, at least she was there. We came to an agreement about practising. Rachel or I, or Sophie, could be making music while the others did something else. There's always some theory or essays or something. plus the cooking. We took it in turns if we were here together, but usually we just did our own.'

I nodded sympathetically, and let her talk.

'But now she'll never come back. We'll never argue again over whose turn it is to wash the mugs. We'll never share practice together, nor...'

The list would have gone on, only Toyah gave way to a burst of anguished tears, sobbing and grabbing tissues to soak up the tears and runny nose.

When she calmed down, we discussed the likely eviction and the need for her to look for somewhere else to live. Somewhere with room to practise as well as study, sleep and entertain.

'I'm afraid my mother has moved in, otherwise you could have had our sofa. David and I are out for most of the day so you would have had the flat to yourself. I'm so sorry not to be of help. But I'll help you look for somewhere.'

She took my hand and pressed it in gratitude. Poor girl had no-one else, it seems.

I promised Toyah that, if she put in a couple of hours practice, I would stay there and go with her to the concert and escort her home again. She was relieved and grateful. That was what was needed. I was about to ask why having Rachel present would not have been just as good, when the young woman arrived. She came straight through and dropped off her bulging plastic bags of groceries on two of the kitchen chairs. She glanced quickly at Toyah, seemed hardly to notice me, retreated along the hallway and went upstairs. There had been no word, no smile nor any sign of emotion about her.

'Well', I asked Toyah. 'Is she always like that, or is she upset at what happened to Sophie?'

According to Toyah, Rachel rarely smiled. She hardly spoke, except when it was necessary. When she did, it was not always to say something pleasant.

'She can be a bit, well, a lot, abrupt. I think she may be shy. Or something.' Toyah's excuse for her. I just found her rude. But then I did not know her. As Nana Ivy often says, 'To know all is to forgive all.' I don't think she knew that came from the pen of the redoubtable Madame de Staël, friend of Fanny Burney, but simply that it saved her and me from a lot of prejudiced thinking.

'Has Rachel spoken to the police yet?' I asked, wondering if David had interviewed her.

'No, she's going in this afternoon.'

Good luck David.

'Will you be looking for somewhere to live together again?'

'Oh no, ' she almost laughed. 'Rachel can afford something better than I can, although she is going back to Leeds. Packing it in here. Sophie's death has really knocked her for six – although you might not think so. I can tell,' she said, 'that she's really cut up. Her parents may be coming down at the weekend, and helping her move back home. She told me that they do not want her staying in the house where someone was, like, killed – you know what I mean. Maybe they think she'll be next.'

I chivvied Toyah into the music room and asked her to play for me the pieces she was due to play that evening. I sat and listened for a while, while I could hear Rachel moving around the kitchen, putting away the shopping and popping something into the microwave. When Rachel passed through the hallway to go back upstairs, I moved into the kitchen as Toyah was obviously sufficiently absorbed in practising –

stopping from time to time to repeat phrases of music with which she was dissatisfied. I took out my folder and set to work on the kitchen table, accompanied by tinkling keyboard music drifting in from the next room.

At five o'clock, Toyah gave up and came into the kitchen. Just then we heard Rachel leaving the house.

'So you don't tell each other what you're doing?' I asked.

'No, not with Rachel. Sophie and I did.'

Mistake, that almost brought on a fresh outpouring of tears.

I bustled about noisily, while Toyah put on her makeup and got ready into her black performance clothes. I put together some bits and pieces, having already found where the spaghetti was stored. A tin of tomatoes, some capers and left-over vegetables, cut small, and a sprinkling of Parmesan provided a makeshift supper, which we hastily swallowed and then put the dirty plates to soak in the sink. We hurried to the underground station and took a crowded tube to Warren Street station, almost running the last stretch along Marylebone Street.

I had time to wait, while Toyah went backstage. When the time came, I felt the pride of an aunt or an older sister to see 'my' Toyah cross the stage to a beautifully decorated harpsichord, take a bow along with the slightly-built blonde young singer, and sit at the stool and play. The performance was entrancing. The singer, sang with a confidence and tonal quality beyond her years. The accompaniment was equally accomplished and the show ended all too soon. I was relieved that Toyah felt able to smile at the applause and look as if nothing had been troubling her. I wondered if any of the audience had any idea of what she had been going through.

I waited while the audience dispersed and the performers emerged from having received the congratulations of the singer's tutors.

The fact that the two young women were at different institutions did not matter at all. They were old boarding-school friends, having both achieved Specialist Music Scholarships to Wells Cathedral School, so had known each other for years.

Toyah introduced me to Laura, and I shook the singer's hand with the sense that one day I would drop into conversation that I had met this star before she was 'discovered'.

Toyah invited Laura to come home with us, which she instantly accepted. Returning to empty digs after an exhilarating performance can emotionally deflate. We took a taxi altogether, with Laura in her stylish long evening dress and carrying her change of clothes with her. On the way, she asked Toyah how much she knew of Sophie's death and of the investigation.

Toyah told her of my connection with the leader of the police investigation team. Laura looked thoughtful and turned to gaze out of the cab window. Toyah and I to exchanged glances. Then Laura turned and said that she might have something to tell the police that she has never told anyone.

'But,' she faltered, 'it may not be at all relevant. It may not even concern Sophie.'

'Well, try me,' I urged, curious to a fault. 'Tell me when we get in, and I'll let you know if you should go to the police with it.'

The rest of the journey passed in silence. I settled the fare, and Toyah led us into the house.

We sat at the kitchen table and Toyah soon produced three steaming mugs and opened a packet of chocolate digestives.

'Well,' Laura began, at my prompting. 'It may be nothing, but Sophie and I had the same piano teacher for a time. We both lived in Norwich. Well, I lived in the city and Sophie lived in a massive house in the countryside not far away. We found out that connection that time I came here after singing in the gala, d'you remember?'

Toyah did, and chuckled for a moment at some memory.

'Well, that piano teacher, Mr Smith-Humphries, well...'
Her voice tailed off.

'Go on,' I encouraged.

'Well, he did something, you know. Actually he used to do it a lot.'

My stomach flipped.

'What, exactly? You'll have to tell someone, and it might as well be me, right now.'

I could not let her stop now.

'He used to touch me. First it was simply to help me put my arms and hands in the right place on the keyboard, then his hands went further south, if you get my meaning?'

I did. 'How old were you?'

'From when I was about nine until I went to Wells, at about 12. He was the best piano teacher in East Anglia, or so everyone thought. I went to him twice a week for an hour, and he touched me, not every time, but, say, every other time. He would take my panties down, and he made me touch him.' She shuddered.

We did not need to know any more.

'He told me to keep quiet about it as other people would not understand and would think I was making it up... I know, I know.'

'But there's been so much publicity about that kind of abuse! How did you not want to tell someone before now?'

'I don't know. Maybe I thought that other kinds of abuse were far worse – real penetrative sex, that kind of thing. I don't know. I just didn't want to talk about it. You know, by talking about it, people might imagine what it was like, and that's really, really embarrassing.'

I attempted to reassure her and Toyah looked on with concern and a furrowed brow, putting her arm round her friend's shoulder. In all the years together at Wells, she had never heard this. I guessed Laura was still a virgin. She had an innocence about her, a touching naïvity.

'What happened to this man? Do you know?'

'No, since leaving to go to Wells, when I got the scholarship, I never went back to him. I don't know if he's still there, or what. I had a singing teacher too but she was lovely, and I've kept in touch with her. She comes to some of my concerts, which is really sweet of her. All the way from Norwich.'

'Do you think – do you know if this Smith-Humphries ever tried it on with Sophie?'

'No, I don't. Except once, when I mentioned his name, she went "Yuk!" That's all. But I felt she wanted to change the subject, so we talked about her cello teacher – a real character! Everyone knew him in Norwich.'

Yuk wasn't a lot to go on, but enough to start enquiries. I knew that David would be really interested, so I took Laura's contact details. She agreed to speak to the police so long as it was my husband. She asked me to tell him in advance all that she had told me so that she did not have to go through it all again. I promised. She changed out of her evening clothes into her jeans and I paid for her taxi home, then flagged one down for me too.

Chapter 8

I TOOK DELIGHT in letting David know this possible development.

'Hey, I'll have to get you co-opted onto the force!' he quipped. 'Consultant detective! But I agree, it's a possible lead. It could be that Sophie was onto him, and he had to silence her. It is certainly worth pursuing.'

The next morning, Norfolk police were on to Smith-Humphries like dogs after a hare. Hearing from another force, and the Met in particular, of a child-abuser on their patch was a humiliation they needed to redeem. They had to show the City boys that they could respond with model diligence and speed in such a possible headline-grabbing situation.

They soon found that the alleged suspect was still teaching children on a one-to-one basis throughout Norwich and surrounding area. If he was still abusing, he had to be stopped, and brought to justice. However, Smith-Humphris was not in when they called.

Neighbours had not seen him recently, and calls to his telephone went unanswered. But the Norfolk cops vowed to leave no stone unturned, and no CCTV camera film unviewed.

The Met's technical team came up first with a development. On Smith-Humphries' webpage and social network sites were things that should not have been there. Across his home page, in bright red letters, as if they had been stamped on, were the words, 'Paedo alert!' Not something that you would advertise yourself.

On his social network sites were the expected notices of concerts that various pupils were playing in, and accounts of successes in piano exams. But that was not all.

David emailed me, he was quite excited.

'Re: S-H. Guess what? On S-H's social media sites: from '#avengingangel' – series of scurrilous and threatening blogs, downright nasty. Started mid-October, 100s, e.g "You pervy bastard. You deserve to have your willy boiled in oil. I hope worms eat your eyes and all your fingers burn slowly." Nice! Noticed something, this troll, as well as vivid imagination, can spell! Most can't.

See you later, have fun, love,

David.'

Was Sophie the troll? Was she seeking revenge or could she have been a blackmailer? David could not wait to get Smith-Humphries in an interview room. More research was needed. Had the creep gone missing or just taken some time off? Had he been in

London over the date of the killing? Had his bank account shown large withdrawals recently? If so, who received them? Sophie's bank account statements showed no significant activity, so maybe there was another person involved, or she was clever at hiding money. Maybe Smith-Humphries paid in cash, if it was blackmail.

Meantime, David's team ploughed on taking statements, holding interviews and generally sleuthing, but this paedo phile connection gave them a clearer sense of direction.

My world revolved as normal. By re-checking some references, I finished the talk I was to give at Chawton House Library, the actual home of Jane Austen's brother.

Lucky Edward Austen had been adopted as a child into a wealthy but childless branch of the family. He inherited and lived in the Manor House at Chawton, and invited his sister Jane to visit, write and dine there, having installed her and their mother in a little worker's cottage in the village.

Like a character in a 'pretend' game (such as filled my childhood's – and not just childhood's – leisure hours) I imagine myself as the Divine Jane, strolling through the front door of this remarkable four-square country house with its long drive and sweeping views of the countryside.

Bought and renovated in the twentieth-century by an American aficionado and collector of women's literature pre-1900, this benefactress had left her library to be a permanent depository and study-centre. It is managed by the University of Southampton, and the whole house is known as The Chawton House Library.

Although I had been a visitor and occasional reader there as a student, I had not so far been invited to be one of their distinguished speakers. Delighted to be so honoured, I hoped to make a good impression so that I might be invited back. My dream would be to take a sabbatical and to stay there as a Visiting Scholar. With David's blessing, of course.

I trawled back through my email Inbox to re-read the invitation from The Library, and was reminded that mine was one of a series on the contribution of the Burney Family to literature and music history. There had already been a talk on the novelist Sarah Harriet Burney, and mine would be on her more famous sister, Fanny – novelist, playwright, journal-keeper and letter-writer.

Then I felt a sudden frisson of excitement. I noticed who else would be delivering a lecture that season. The week after mine, the talk would be given by the latest of that series of mature lovers of poor dead Sophie, the American Dr Augustus P. Oakwood.

His lecture was on Dr Charles Burney, music historian, composer and musician. Naturally, he would mention the Haydn connection with Dr Charles Burney, particularly in the light of his groundbreaking discovery of the unfinished oratorio. This discovery was the talk of the town – well, at least of the musical buffs – and we were all waiting for his book to be published telling all about it. It was a researcher's equivalent of a lottery win, to make such a discovery. Apparently the unfinished oratorio could well have been as great as both *The Creation* and *The Seasons*. Maybe another scholar could flesh it out as someone did with Mozart's unfinished Requiem.

The only shame was that the notable Haydn scholar Howard Robbins Landon was no longer alive. He had rescued and recorded many forgotten works by Haydn and knew more about him than probably anyone else. He would have been thrilled with this discovery, akin almost to finding a lost work of Shakespeare, but died five years before it hit the headlines.

I checked my diary and found that, by moving one evening tutorial to the following night, if the student were willing, I could attend this talk. Apart from the subject-matter, the gossip in me was agog to meet this man who had found young Sophie so attractive. Was he a sleezeball who had enticed Sophie with expensive gifts, or a handsome fellow with whom it was easy for a youthful woman to fall in love?

When I next emailed David, he confirmed that Oakwood had been interviewed by the team. Later that night, as we lay warming the bed together, David commissioned me to find out all I could about this American scholar.

'I'm sure you will do just as well, if not better, than my highly trained and professional squad,' he murmured, while gently nibbling my ear. This confidence in me was sweet of him, and, if his purpose was in softening me up for a night of passion, it worked. Least said...

Chapter 9

Thursday

THERE WERE MORE AUDITIONS the next day. Once we cast the plays, and briefed the backstage staff, the directorial team gave out copies of the texts for the cast to learn over the Christmas vacation. The team then withdrew to the college canteen and, round the table, in between bites from our tortilla wraps, we drew up a provisional rehearsal schedule for the new year.

The 'we' consisted of Dorothy, an elderly but still energetic staff member from Theatre Studies; Michael, a postgrad in Performance Studies, and me as advisor on period and literary issues. Dorothy was in overall control, but Michael was to do most of the actual work – and benefit from it for his PhD. He was gorgeous, sunny natured and witty, and I tried not to let it show too much that I thought so. He was more Hollywood than academia and had sufficient numbers of adoring students, both boys and girls, following in his wake. One day I expect his will be a big name.

The police investigation seemed to be stalling, although the disappearance of the piano teacher was taking up more of the team's attention. They were mystified by the identity of the social media troll, as no amount of technical delving seemed able to discover it.

The Norfolk police were able to provide a date and time after which Smith-Humphries went totally missing. On October 27th his car was picked up on a CCTV camera heading east just outside Norwich. If he were making for London, the car was likely to have reappeared on another camera somewhere on the M11, but it did not. There had been no on-line or telephone bookings of train or coach tickets to London for some weeks, either. Nor had his credit or debit card been used since the 27th. He was making it difficult to be traced.

We knew he was devious, as he had been able to cover his tracks as a child molester for at least a decade. Such a mind would devise ways of disappearing with equal facility. I could tell David was frustrated by the lack of progress by the tone of his voice.

Curiosity drew me back to Toyah's house again after work. She had mentioned that Sophie's boyfriend Matt Brizzi had arranged to be there to pick up some things which had either belonged to him or were owned jointly by him and

Sophie. The police had finished with the house and all the rooms had been opened again. I wanted to meet the boyfriend. Boyfriend, partner, husband – so often a female victim's assailant. Also I wanted to give some comfort to Toyah who was finding it difficult to concentrate on her work.

When I arrived, Rachel opened the door to me, with the same emotionless expression she had worn the previous time. She had looks that could have been attractive – delicately built, with large dark eyes and sleek black hair drawn back into a tight little bun high up on the back of her head. But they were spoilt by such a dull expression – from disappointment with life in general, reaction to the tragic death of her housemate, or simply from a sense of superiority? I could not tell and didn't really care.

She left me to find Toyah sitting at the table in the unlit kitchen, obviously crying. She quickly stood up, as if I had discovered her doing something reprehensible, and turned on the light. Then I could see the ravages of tears around her eyes.

'It's all right to cry, ' I said in an attempt at consolation. 'What really gets me,' she replied, 'is that Sophie had no-one really to grieve for her. Her mother's miles away, and last I heard was terminally ill. Who else really cares?'

That started her off again. I drew her into the now-liberated sitting room to continue the conversation. Even the slight change of scene would, I hoped, be sufficient to break the current cycle of thoughts and tears. I pulled an armchair round, so that we could face each other, the better to chat confidentially.

'Had she no aunts, or cousins?'

None, apparently. The father had left home years before and died since. The mother had herself been an only child, and had inherited the fortune left by her own parents. There was one brother of Sophie's late father, but he too had been off the scene for years.

'At least there is Matt, Matt Brizzi, isn't it? The boyfriend. The one who's coming round later?'

'Sure, he seems fond of her. They were close, good friends as well as lovers. Although', she added ruefully, 'Sophie did seem rather to dominate him.'

'Was he her first? Was she keen on him?'

'Not her first, but she really was fond of him. They shared everything, even thought alike, both laughing when no-one caught the joke, that sort of thing. Apart from him, she didn't hang out with other students. She preferred older men. She said they're more sophisticated – more like the people at home, in Barbados. She wouldn't be ... unkind. She could even be really generous sometimes, to people she liked.'

'She must have liked you. I believe she paid most of your rent, yours and Rachel's?

'Yeah, true. Mind you, Rachel and I did most of the chores – the shopping, cooking and washing up. Sophie paid for a cleaner once a week to do the vacuuming and heavy cleaning. I've stopped her coming in now. Can't afford it. We all do our own laundry. Rachel's parents, for once, provided the tumble drier. of course, she wants it back now.'

'So she's really going?'

'Yeah. She's off to Leeds in a few days' – to her boyfriend's flat.'

From Toyah's tone, it did not seem that Rachel would be much missed, although she had agreed to pay her portion of the rent to the end of the year. Sophie had everything that, according to Toyah, Rachel lacked, in spades. She had personality. She was bright and sunny, at least to those she wanted to impress. Most fellow students and staff at the music college rarely saw this side to her nature, and thought her rather stuck up.

'She could be a bitch, too,' Toyah had to admit. 'She would suddenly explode with rage at anything. She had this horribly snobby way of saying "little people" about people doing their jobs, especially if any slighted her.'

So who is perfect?

'There were times when I was really afraid of her,' Toyah added, quietly. 'She had dark moods when no-one could approach, not even Rachel, or Matt.'

She paused, remembering.

'Sometimes too, although she knew more about the world than I do, even though I'm like four years older, she could behave like a child. You know, how children can laugh easily or cry. She could be like that – hugging and kissing and smiling. Or suddenly burst into tears.'

She was certainly a complex character. Musically, as Toyah explained, she was really accomplished, a natural performer with seemingly no nerves. She was happy to play along with Toyah, and on occasion Rachel would join in – the three of them making music purely for their own enjoyment. These were the happiest times for Toyah, the times she would treasure.

Toyah reached a point of resignation, almost serenity, when loud knocks at the front door announced the arrival of the bereaved boyfriend.

Again, Rachel, leaving the kitchen where she was eating, played doorkeeper. Matt walked confidently into the sitting room but then seemed a little taken aback to find Toyah was not alone.

'Hi, I'm Matt. I've come to get some things. I left stuff here...'

His voice trailed off. I looked for the arrogant swagger that David had described, but failed to find it. 'That's fine. Toyah said you would. Pleased to meet you. I'm Julia, doing some work with Toyah on her thesis.'

'Oh, yes. Dr Deane. You teach at Queen's. Toyah has talked about you.' We shook hands formally while I remained seated.

'I'm sorry,' I offered. 'Do get what you came for. Toyah and I were just talking about Sophie. I am sorry for your loss.' The usual useful cliché.

Then Toyah stood up and started to select CDs and DVDs from the rack next to the fireplace.

'It's OK,' urged Matt, moving towards her. 'I can do that, thanks.'

He picked out half a dozen more, stuffing them into a small backpack while the two of us watched. Then Toyah remembered her hostess manners and, after offering to make coffee, went out to do so. Matt moved to the bookcase of novels and took a couple off the shelf, putting them with the tapes. Then he looked around the desk, in it and under.

'Have you seen a laptop? It should be here, somewhere. Maybe it's upstairs.'

'No, it won't be,' I offered. 'The police will have it. They'll be checking it.'

I almost blurted out that they would be looking for signs of trolling, of any evidence that emails had been sent to anyone in Norwich, or certain messages posted on social media sites.

Being close to police investigations was interesting, but also dangerous. I could not let anyone know how much I knew. David had confided in me information that was meant to be kept strictly within the police service. I only just averted the disaster.

'Oh yes,' he said with narrowing eyes. 'You're married to that D.I. – the one who interviewed me after Sophie was killed. Has he found who did it yet? Do they know?'

He looked as if he could mete out his own justice if the accused were before him. I made some non-committal noises and was relieved when Toyah arrived with three mugs of brown liquid. We all sat down. I asked if he had any ideas of why anyone would want to kill his girlfriend, and his demeanour changed.

He sighed deeply and almost tearfully described a girl who was a paragon of virtue and a terrific partner. Allowing for grief distorting memory and endowing lost loved ones with unlikely perfections, I believed that the boy had really loved Sophie and that his misery was genuine. I crossed him off my list of suspects, and began to feel sorry for him and even like him a little.

I know.

Being charming is no barrier to being a killer – and seven women a month, on average, fall victim to domestic violent deaths in the UK. Some of their partners must have been thought charming and wonderful at some stage in the relationship.

However, to me, Matt did seem genuine. Or else he was a brilliant actor.

I asked him more about himself and he opened up quite lucidly. He had hoped to marry Sophie, but she was not as keen as he was on such a total commitment. She wanted to develop her career, he reflected. She had an amazing talent, he insisted, with a great future ahead of her. Almost in tears now, he confided that, although they had known each other for less than two years, it was as if they had been together for ever.

'Even when she went with other men?' I inquired somewhat insensitively. It fortunately did not faze him.

'Yes, even then. I knew she did. It was something we arranged together, really.'

This was a surprisingly candid admission.

'She didn't care for them. They were older and seem to fall for her. She really played with them. Got what she could from them and then left. It was their own fault. They did the running, she just acted as the quarry, and paid them back by being nice to them.'

'How nice?' I was gruesomely curious.

'Well, you know. She kind of, like, slept with them. Well, yes, she did. But it didn't mean anything. Not to her, and not to them either. They just wanted her because she was young and pretty and.... And she played up to that. So everyone was happy.'

'Were you, really?' I was probing.

'Well...OK, not really. But that was her, that was Sophie. It was a game to her, but with me it was real. I know that. She told me about them, but not them about me. When we were married, she would stop that, and settle for just me. But now I'll never know.'

When Matt left, I reassured Toyah that there was someone to grieve properly for Sophie, and that was Matt. She was comforted, I do believe, and I left her promising that she would do some research into the Haydn correspondence with Dr Charles Burney so that I would have some further background to hand when I went to hear Sophie's ex-plaything, at Chawton House Library.

When I got home, about nine o'clock, Helena was still out and David had texted to say he was busy and not to expect him until about ten.

I put a few eatables together for a light supper for us all, and watched some television. Helena returned shortly after I had settled, and as she had not buzzed to be allowed in through the front door, I realized where she had been – in the downstairs flat.

In fact, she was there, she admitted, nearly every day. Far from Mr Hobson being appalled by her, he actually kept asking for her, inviting her into his apartment to keep him company. I think he thought of her as an exotic distraction in his otherwise dull, lonely life.

They even went out together, to the park, to the local shops and had plans to go to the theatre. Helena had not said anything before, but I had noticed new items being added to her wardrobe. She had opened a bank account with some money Nana Ivy had sent her, and I offered to add to it. There should be a pension somewhere too that she needed to find out about. I said that I would help her over that, too. At one time she would have told me not to meddle. Funny how situations change attitudes.

This night, she wanted to spill the beans. She looked flushed and was smiling rather more than customarily. Apparently Mr Hobson had complimented her on her interesting conversation.

'You never converse interestingly with me!' I complained.

'That's because you've always got David, or your work or something,' retorted Helena, rather hurt by my comment. 'I have wanted to talk with you ever since I came, but with this murder business and everything, well, you've not had time for me.'

I was stung by the justice of her remark.

'All right. David's not back for half an hour or so, so let's talk now.'

'You can't just turn it on... But, all right, tell me. Why did you marry David, especially as you weren't even pregnant? And why no children? Is there something wrong with either of you?'

Had it not been Helena, I would have been deeply offended by this full-frontal attack. But I saw it coming. I always sensed that she thought I had done something stupid in getting married. Her not coming to the wedding on the flimsy excuse of there being no transport available was a bold statement of her disapproval. I had been relieved on the day itself by her non-arrival as I had dreaded the sort of fight on the day that was brewing now. I was also glad to be on my own now, and not to have this conversation with David present.

'First, I married David because I loved him. We love each other.'

Snort. 'Huh, but you don't have to...'

'Then we *do* intend to have children, but it hasn't been the right time yet. I want to get this college year over, finish some writing I'm doing and see through the Burney plays the college is putting on. We are hoping to start a family later next year. And there's nothing wrong with either of us! Anyway, David is putting in for a transfer next year and then we hope to have a house to live in. We can't really bring up a child in this flat. I'm sure Mr Hobson wouldn't want to be wakened up by baby screams all night!'

'But marriage is so oppressive,' Helena spouted, sounding still the rebellious teenager she seemed always to be. 'There are so many other ways of living than chaining yourself to one man all your life. Look at the divorce rate! Facts bear it out. If we were made to be committed for life to just one other person we would not be so ready, as a species, to jump ship. It's human nature. You can't fight it. I suppose it's your Nana Ivy who fed your mind with all that "marriage" stuff. Makes you feel respectable, does it?'

By now I was fighting anger. How dare she challenge me like that when she could see how David and I got on happily together? We were not shackled, not victims of any oppressive regime. We were mutually supportive, finding comfort and solace from each other, being affirmed by the vows we had taken, knowing that, for each other, we were prepared to forego all others. Of course it was not all plain sailing, but. ...

Just then my mobile made that *Pingy* call tone and I was relieved to have to take it into the bedroom to answer it in private.

It was Toyah. She sounded quite shaken and scared.

'I'm so sorry to bother you, Dr Deane,' she said quaveringly. 'But I'm a bit worried.'

'It's OK, Toyah. What's this about?'

'There's someone outside. Just by the front gate. He's been there for ages. Just keeps looking up at the windows, downstairs and upstairs.'

'Where are you?' Daft question.

'I'm upstairs in Sophie's bedroom. The light's off so I can see him but hope he can't see me. Rachel noticed him first.'

'What does he look like? Have you called the police?'

'No, not yet. Rachel said not to bother unless he does

something. He's old, middle aged, and big – tall and sort of heavy.'

'And what is he wearing?' It was all I could think of to ask.

'He's got a thick coat, padded type I think, and has one of those lumberjack sort of hats on – flaps front and sides, and flat on top. It's too dark to see him properly. The street lights are behind and to the side of him. I can just see the silhouette. He's blocking the light. Ah,' she added, with sudden relief. 'He's just moved off. Gone now. Oh, I am sorry to bother you. It's probably nothing.'

I told her not to worry, and that I would tell David myself as I expected him home at any moment.

Chapter 10

DAVID TOOK THE SIGHTING seriously and arranged for a patrol car to pass by the house in Fulham on a frequent, but irregular, basis. He discussed with his sergeant whether a full witness protection scheme should be put in place, but they agreed to see if the man appeared again or anything else take place of a sinister nature.

Witness protection takes up huge chunks of police budget and has to be approved by various higher authorities. And so far as they knew, neither Toyah nor Rachel was a witness to anything significant. He agreed though that the sighting was potentially worrying and ordered that the team stepped up their search for the missing Norwich piano teacher. That was their preferred line of enquiry for the time being, although other options were being kept open.

I asked what progress had been made on finding the mother's partner, and the thwarted Russian cello buyer.

Both had been traced, but neither had yet been interviewed.

The Russian police had located their countryman, and were waiting for the necessary paperwork to be arranged between the Metropolitan Police, the Foreign Office and *Minyust*, their Ministry of Justice. Only then would they take him to one of their police stations for questioning by their own police.

The mother's partner had flown back to Barbados from London on the second of November. The Barbadian police were preparing to take him in for questioning, but wanted David to be there in person. Ha! He was not likely to refuse a chance to go to the sunny island on a cold November day. He had put in the necessary travel requests and was just waiting for clearance.

I then asked about Sophie's former older lovers, the famous musician and the American scholar. David had not thought either of them worth pursuing, at least at that time, especially as the piano teacher was looking more and more likely as the suspect. His bank account had shown significant withdrawals over the past few months.

However, although Sophie and he had a shared past, and she had obviously thought him high on the 'Yuk' scale, it was Laura, not the victim, who had brought him to the attention of the police. There was a worrying lack of any evidence connecting Smith-Humphries with Sophie over the whole of the past decade.

Suspicion had first fallen on her as the social networking troll and website vandal, simply because she had been the murder victim. However, no evidence had been found on her laptop, or anything else to suggest she was so proficient in computer matters to be capable of doing this. Nor had her bank account shown unusual deposits recently. Her current account was healthy and deposit accounts had long held more funds than either David and I possessed between us. Yet the possibility remained strong that somehow there was a blackmailing scam that had resulted in the death of the young woman. Until Smith-Humphries was found, no-one could know for sure.

Suspicion continued to fall on him. Could he have been the man outside the house in Fulham? Why on earth would he be there? He, if he were the culprit, would know that Sophie was dead. So why risk discovery, when he had been so careful not to be found up until then? Presumably that applied to whoever was the killer. Only a complete fool would put himself at such a risk as to haunt the victim's residence. Was it just ghoulish curiosity that made a stranger stand and stare at the house of a murder victim? But who, outside those who needed to, knew where to find it?

The press had obliged in keeping the identity of the 'Hallowe'en Victim' secret. David had asked each interviewee, and the Director had requested all students at the RCM, not to disclose Sophie's name to anyone from the media or indeed to anyone beyond the investigation. The fewer people who knew the better. The excuse given was that the girl's mother deserved to be told before finding it out, and that her gravely ill condition made that difficult for the present.

Really it was in the hope that the perpetrator would give him or herself away somehow by disclosing more than they would have otherwise known. It happened in fiction. Why not now? Ah, because reality is always more complex.

Anyway, the next day Toyah was less fearful of seeing the scary stranger again and more concerned at finding somewhere else to live. The landlord had been very decent, allowing her to stay on until the end of the year, when the contract would have been up for renewal, and he accepted the reduction in rent.

Rachel's father and boyfriend arrived on the Sunday and removed her goods into their capacious hired van, including the tumble drier. Her father wrote a cheque, made out to the landlord, settling up her rent, less her share of the returnable deposit, to the end of December. The two men, as taciturn as Rachel herself, simply did what they needed to and left with Rachel, her books, instruments, clothes and kitchen items.

The spaces where her dishes, mugs and pans had been gave Toyah a pang of unexpected sadness, even more than Rachel's actual absence. They reminded her that half of the items remaining belonged to someone who would never be able to take them away, would never use them here or in another home.

That Saturday I spent on doing some of the paperwork that used to be done, in the good old days, by numerous administration staff, departmental secretaries and other personnel now deemed to be redundant by people who had never actually had to teach and do research.

I spent the remaining time on preparing lectures while trying to avoid my mother. I did not want to continue the tired old conversation about marriage, nor begin to tread on the ground of why I became a Catholic. That would be next, I sensed.

Chapter 11

Sunday

THE NEXT DAY I INVITED Toyah round for Sunday lunch, mainly as she would otherwise have been on her own, but also in the hope that Helena might behave herself in front of a young stranger. I went to the 8.30 Low Mass to give myself some time to shop and prepare the lunch, while David put in some more hours at work.

He and Toyah arrived at about the same time, one o'clock, and we all went directly to the table. I provided a warming Jerusalem artichoke soup followed by a root vegetable gratin, inspired by a Rachel Demuth recipe, and baked apples stuffed with sultanas and marmalade, with a home-made egg custard.

David opened two bottles of Cotswold *No Brainer* cider, bought last time we went together to visit David's family near Tewkesbury, the small medieval market town in north Gloucestershire.

Over lunch Helena was actually charming, asking Toyah questions politely but with apparent interest, about her studies, her family in Barbados, and what she intended to do once she had her doctorate. David spoke little about the investigation but mentioned that he would soon have to go to Barbados for a few days. He asked Toyah various questions about the island.

I prattled on merrily about looking forward to visiting the house at Chawton with the close connection with Jane Austen, and its amazing collection of first editions and other prized volumes. I hinted hard about the amount of work I had to do, and about how far behind I had fallen with a paper for a literary journal I had barely begun to write, in the hope that Helena would realize I needed space and peace in which to work.

I was used to bringing home as much work as I could, as I was not good at working in the university library – the books around me proving too great a distraction, not to mention the sound of tapping keyboards. I avoided working in my college study too, as my peace would be interrupted by colleagues and students. As my room faced the busy Kingsway, the sound of traffic annoyed me, despite being six floors up. Also after hours, the cleaners would come bustling in, or call and chat to each other just outside the door.

I enjoyed working at home, spreading out papers and books, with gentle background music playing from my CD collection. I felt that the instrumental music of Rameau, Vivaldi and Mozart enabled me to concentrate at my best.

Then Toyah suggested something that would, as the horrible expression goes, kill two birds with one stone.

'When you're away, David, could Dr Deane, Julia, sorry, stay over at mine, using either Sophie's or Rachel's room? I hate being on my own in the house. I'll be out all day at college. But at night, it'd be great to, like, have some company in the house.'

'Has that bloke been round again?' asked David, frowning.

'No, but I would feel safer'.

I beamed. Helena, too, smiled widely. She was making a habit of looking and being amiable. I had no idea what she was planning to do once I went away overnight, but I could see that the prospect did not displease her. I just hoped that no drunken parties were on her mind. And that she would keep out of my bed, alone or with anyone else. David shrugged, indifferent, looking to me for a response. It suited him well enough.

'The change might do you good, love, and you'd be able to work with no interruption or distraction.'

The deal was struck.

*　　　*　　　*　　　*

David's Barbados trip did not take place for another week, held up by paperwork. The week was one in which not much happened; certainly no progress was reported by him on the Sophie murder case.

Life at home was quiet, with Helena going out for most of the day, coming in late to sleep, and waking after I left each morning. I had a few meetings, notably a fairly alcoholic lunchtime one with Dorothy and handsome Michael. He had brought a friend, Peter, with him to *Bill's,* the Luyten's designed eatery further up Kingsway.

Peter was theatrical to the core, a director of avant-guard dramas in London and New York that tended to flop rather quickly. I feared he would be dismissive of our revival of a couple of eighteenth-century plays that had not seen the light of day until the 1990s. Fanny Burney's father and his friend, known as Daddy Crisp, had prevented one of the plays, *The Witlings* even from being published after it was written in 1779, partly from fear of offending the literary set upon whom they depended for their livelihood, and partly from sensing the impropriety of a woman writing a comedy for the stage.

Peter could not have been more charming, with a disarming humour. He and Michael were obviously 'an item' – news of which would break the hearts of many female students. Dorothy was obviously held in high esteem by both young men, and basked in their admiration. They were warm and attentive to me too, although I had nothing of the track record in theatre that Dorothy enjoyed.

We discussed the casting and general approach to the plays, opting for a period set and costume, as the language and mores of the time would be difficult enough to comprehend without having to make constant mental adjustments if the setting were to be updated. I was relieved as I thought I would have to battle for this, but found I had no need to, in the event. As the plays had been performed but rarely, we were not about to suffer from comparisons.

The weather in the middle of November was unseasonably mild, and Christmas itself was some way off. However, there were not many weeks left of term, and much marking and assessing had to be undertaken. So, apart from eating, sleeping and commuting, my life was taken up solely with work.

Then I got the phone call. David was booked on an evening flight that very day and he had dropped in at home to throw something together and pick up his passport. Helena, he told me, was entertaining a group of elderly men in our living room, all friends of Mr Hobson, with whisky and tea, at two in the afternoon! He was amused. I was appalled. How many riotous soirées had she been hosting in our apartment in our absence? Why were there no women in the group? What were they getting up to?

I caught myself feeling like a Victorian matron, and turned my attention to the offer of the use of Toyah's house for both work and company.

After my last seminar in the afternoon, I spent another hour with the poor bewildered postgrad Tom Jacobs.

As he seemed to have no idea how to go about finding primary source material, I suggested that he made contact with Dr Oakwood at the RCM to find out exactly how he had made the Haydn discovery. It could only help the youngster to know how exciting real original scholarship can be.

I even offered to take him to the talk the American was to give at Chawton, but recommended that he made a point of seeing him first.

Tom is a young man with a permanently worried expression. He wears his hair close-shaven at the sides and back and long, full and curly at the front and on the crown, with black curls tumbling over his forehead, almost obscuring his left eye. With something of a winsome puppy about him he drew on my motherly feelings. I wanted to do what I could to help him. After our hour, I took off for home, now empty of parent and her male coven.

Just as David had done a few hours earlier, I gathered up some overnight things and drove round to the Fulham street where there was an unrestricted parking place, and walked round the corner to Toyah's.

She welcomed me in and took me to Rachel's room, having made up the bed in there. I was glad not to be sleeping in the dead girl's bed, as my imagination overnight would have played a fugue of morbid thoughts.

After a simple, but filling, supper with my young companion, and putting in a couple of hours reading, I went up to bed and Toyah shortly followed to her own. I soon fell into a deep sleep, dreaming of the Moscow metro and David chasing a suspect, who was wearing an oversized astrakhan hat, down ornately decorated corridors one of which curiously opened out onto a tropical beach.

I was just about to join him under a palm tree as we prepared to go for a swim, when I was suddenly aware of Toyah creeping into my room, closing the door quietly behind her. A quick check to convince myself I was not dreaming, when she shushed me and squatted beside my pillows. I could see her form in monochrome, with just enough street lighting illuminating the room. Talking rapidly in a whisper and sounding frightened, she said that she had heard a noise from downstairs.

My pulse went into overdrive and my stomach lurched. Shush.

'Listen!' she commanded. 'There's someone down there. I know there is. D'you hear that?'

There was a definite clunk of something.

'Where's your phone?' I whispered urgently. My first reaction is always to tell the police.

'Downstairs. In my coat pocket. Where's yours?'

Oh God, I left mine in my handbag, and that was also downstairs. What a couple of idiots. We both froze.

Footsteps were quietly but steadily mounting the stairs, getting closer.

Silence.

Fear – chilling, immobilising fear.

Then anger.

'Chair!' I ordered, and Toyah immediately sprang to take the chair from in front of the dressing table and placed in under the handle of the bedroom door. It would not stop a determined intruder, but might made a nervous one think twice before pushing the door open with that behind it.

I was breathing in shallow bursts, far too loudly, although probably inaudible to anyone else. I could also imagine my heart beats to be heard by anyone nearby. Toyah was back beside my bed, and we gripped each other's hands.

'Is there anything here, in this room, we could use as a weapon?' I asked, already knowing the likely answer.

As she was thinking and doubting, I suddenly remembered I had a small bottle of *Marks & Spencer's* Rose Eau de Toilette on the dressing table. I sprang out of bed, took it up, and went to kneel on the chair behind the door.

The sound of heavy steps just outside the door caused my adrenaline levels to shoot up into every cell in my body. The door began to open, slowly, slowly. I could hear the breathing of whoever was making their unwanted entrance. The door pressed against the resistance of the chair, and stopped moving for a moment. Then it was pushed harder and a dark form blocked out the faint light on the landing, caused by the street light coming through the hall window. Just when I thought was the right moment, and judging the position of the intruder's eyes from his general height, I squirted the astringent perfume into them as close as I dared to get.

The resultant oath and short cry of pain told me I had found the mark. His sudden reflexive turning away was all I needed to slam the door shut, replace the chair behind it and sit on it. We heard footsteps, no longer quiet and gentle, but now running, as the man, for to be sure it was a he, made his way out of the house as quickly as he could. Toyah was at the window curtain in two or three light bounds, and drew a space through which she could watch whoever was leaving.

'It's him!' she cried as I joined her, folding open more of the curtain. 'The man who was at the gate the other day!'

We watched as a man, not in his prime, hurried along the path, throwing open the gate, and turning left into the street. Shortly after, we heard the sound of an engine starting and moving off. The man had been wearing dark clothing, with something like a long quilted jacket, and a peaked lumberjack hat, the sort with ear flaps, which seemed to be down over his ears. It had been too difficult to pick out any features, but he seemed heavy set and too old to be a casual burglar. We tend to think of those miscreants as lithe teenaged lads.

We put on the landing light and went downstairs to see what damage had been done. There was none. Although he had had time to go into every room, there was no disturbance, no sign of his having been there.

We both collected our mobiles, and as I was the first one ready, I made the 999 call. I reported the incident and let the duty officer know the significance of the house involved, and of Toyah's involvement with the recent 'Hallowe'en Murder' victim.

I so wanted David to be home. He would have been round in a second. As it was, I had no wish to try to contact him, mid-flight over the Atlantic somewhere. I guessed it would alarm him, and frustrate him that he could not do anything to console me personally.

We got dressed and waited up for a police patrol car to deliver a couple of uniformed officers. They came after just a few minutes. One was young and black, the other older and of Pakistani appearance. Both were attentive and pleasant, reassuring us that the intruder was unlikely to make another appearance.

I was a bit worried that I might have blinded him, and be accused of using unnecessary violence, but again the two coppers were reassuring. They took statements and asked us not to touch anything downstairs. A forensic scene-of-crime team would be round in the morning. That was more attention than most attempted burglaries would have received, I felt. But the possible link with the murder case gave our case special significance.

A second police car arrived a few minutes later, and a blond woman officer in her thirties emerged.

'Call me Wendy' arranged to stay in the house overnight to allow us some sleep before the SOCO officers arrived. After the original two left, Toyah made tea for the three of us, and we took ours upstairs while Wendy made herself comfortable in an armchair in the sitting room. I slept eventually for barely an hour before the weak November sunshine through the curtain told me it was time to get up.

I rang a colleague from my department, canceled my morning tutorial and apologized for my absence at a meeting that afternoon. I felt I had to stay with Toyah, and be available for any more police enquiries. I had enough work with me to do, so I set to it and the time flew past.

Chapter 12

THE NEXT DAY TOYAH arranged to stay in the RCM's hall of residence, in the guest room reserved for occasional visitors. The hall manager appreciated the need for safe refuge, although was wary that the intruder may be attracted to her establishment. The police assured her that they would patrol the area round the hall with more than usual diligence. They also gave Toyah the number of a direct line, to contact them the moment she detected anything sinister, or even the suspicion of it.

They did not think that I was the target of the burglar's interest, but maybe only the house and possibly Toyah herself. They put a seal on the house and suggested that Toyah stayed away from it for a while. I returned to my flat, once Toyah was settled in her new accommodation.

Helena was home when I arrived, and seemed unnaturally pleased to see me. She insisted on my telling her whatever I knew about the murder case, and the details of the night's uninvited visitor. I felt that, for the first time in my life, I was able to converse with my mother without her taking me to task over my lifestyle or with me doing the same over hers. She seemed interested and made the proper interjections of support and expressions of sympathy that a normal person would do. For once we were behaving like adults, two people sharing something that both could feel similarly about.

The next few days passed in the usual way, with my working either in college or just in the flat, and Helena disappearing downstairs. Her absence enabled me to spread my work over the kitchen table.

The talk for Chawton was prepared, and the day of my talk there arrived. I set out for the Hampshire countryside with delighted anticipation of being received at the historic home of women's literature as an invited contributor.

The event was all that I expected. At the wine reception before the talk, I was surrounded by a group of bright young women postgrads from Southampton University, all eager to learn more about one of the eighteenth century's greatest English writers – if not the greatest. Once we had chatted and laughed together for a time, I did my best to 'work the room' as politicians say.

There was a sprinkling of Burney Society members, always a joy to meet, and some whose profession or occupation had no apparent connection with the subject other than a genuine amateur interest – always encouraging to those of us who toil in academia to provide this interest with new material.

The World According to Julia

I stayed overnight in a four-poster bed in The Stables and breakfasted in a bright and airy conservatory, feeling as happy as it is possible to be on one's own. The scary night was forgotten as I recalled how the talk had gone well, the audience seeming pleased and the organisers enthusiastic. They beamed when I told them I was hoping to return in a week's time to hear Dr Oakwood, and mentioned my plan to bring Tom with me.

I rang him from my breakfast table to see how he had got on with the amorous American. He answered rather drowsily and said that the interview had gone fairly well, discussing Haydn and his music, but about the discovery of the oratorio he could not get much out of him.

I have known that avoidance problem before, with occasional insecure academics being wary of young researchers probing and prying a little too far. They sometimes seem to fear their work could be overtaken before they had really milked it of all its present value. I mused about how record-breakers in sport must feel about up-and-coming competitors taking the shine off their achievements before the applause had even subsided. From an academic that seemed pathetic, but then the American university scene is so competitive that that the pressure ther is probably even more intense and stressful than in the UK.

I mentioned the forthcoming Oakwood talk at Chawton, describing the place to him and offered to drive him down, As it would be deep winter with possibly poor road conditions, I would also arrange for us both to overnight in a cheap bed and breakfast near by. Two rooms, I almost said, but stopped before embarrassing him.

He sounded enthusiastic, so I asked him to write up a report of his work so far and of the interview with the professor. We would meet for a tutorial after the Chawton talk, and could talk together on the way down. At last Tom seemed to have caught some glimmer of light. He promised to pursue the matter and try to soften Oakwood up somewhat in order to probe further into how such a discovery of an unknown manuscript could be made. I was delighted when he even suggested flying over to Austria in the new year to visit the schloss where the manuscript had been found. It pleased me immensely to hear Tom's new tone of hope and burgeoning commitment to his project, and imagined it could do nothing but good.

I drove home through the Hampshire countryside and London suburbs, avoiding the M25, and Helena and I had a talk about women's involvement in literature at a time when they could not make their voices heard in any other forum. She was delighted with a find she had made in one of the books I had brought home.

'Guess what?' she asked with a gleam. 'I've been looking at this play, *Rover* by Aphra Benn, written, what? In the seventeenth century?'

'1677', I informed her. 'What of it?'

'Well, there's a woman in it called Hellena, but with two 'l's, and one called Angellica Bianca, a high-class tart. She gives a great put-down to the double standards of the time. "Who made the laws by which you judge me? Men!" Isn't that brilliant? All that time ago, and yet men and women are still judged by different criteria.'

I considered we had made some progress since those days, although she was right that there are still in use words to describe a promiscuous woman that would not be applied to a similar man.

And yes, the laws are still, to a large extent, made by men and therefore in their interests.

Then, as I feared, the conversation suddenbly lurched towards Catholicism. My chosen Church's exclusion of women from decision-making was not something that I was delighted to discuss, so I suggested a cup of tea and snack while we waited for David to come home.

David returned with an interesting development in the murder investigation. Despite jet lag and with too little time on the island paradise to take in the sun, he was bright and keen to share his news with me. And Helena, who now insisted on being included in our conferences. That dampened his enthusiasm somewhat, as he could not be sure how confidentially she would keep his reports. He acquiesced, on obtaining assurances from her, supported by my desire to give my mother a sense of inclusion in the hope that our newly close relationship would develop.

I was so pleased to see him, I grinned idiotically and laughed a little too readily at his jokes. I wanted him so badly and could barely wait for him to tell us his tale so that we could go to bed and lie close, feeling the warmth of each other's bodies. Still, he needed first, after a welcoming hug, a meal, a stiff drink and the chance to tell us how about his flights and interviews.

All had gone smoothly, and the local police were as obliging as could be. He had seen the mother, no longer lying prone and unconscious, but sitting up in bed and demanding to know the details of her darling child's hideous death.

My sensitive husband had spared Mrs Anderson as much as he could, but it is not possible to wrap up the facts of murder in any language that really soothes. He lied about the girl not feeling fear and pain. 'All over so quickly', was how he kindly put it.

Apparently the partner, Ivor McShea, had broken the news to her when he felt that she was able to bear it. But hearing it from a London policeman seemed to make it more real, and the poor woman could not hide her grief despite her best efforts to refrain from weeping. She was of the class and tradition which considered it 'bad form' to show too much emotion, and David wished she had just howled with despair rather than struggled with constant self-control.

He described her as a woman in her late fifties, well made-up and coiffed, but looking haggard and thin. She sat up in bed, with a silk sheet up to her waist and wearing a frilly lacy negligée that was almost transparent. She kept sipping iced water from a bed-side glass, which was replenished by the black maid from time to time.

David interviewed the maid, Suzanna, to get some background on the victim's life, but heard nothing more than platitudes and general comments of the 'lovely child' and 'so talented'. The untimely death of her young charge did not appear to have moved her greatly. David assumed that was because she had seen her only during the winter vacations from school and college. But there was a coldness about the maid's response on the subject of Sophie that made him think the young woman may not have been as kind or considerate to the staff as she might have been.

Suzanna did seem genuinely fond of her ailing mistress and approved of her partner, Mister McShea, for giving the lady a new interest in her life. His company really 'bucked her up' was how Suzanna put it.

David's real interest was with McShea. As soon as the man had returned to the island from London in early November, he had arranged a speedy marriage with the older woman. David doubted that it had been or would ever be able to be consummated. But that would not be an issue unless an annulment were sought at some point.

He could see the advantages for the man in this marriage, but failed to see why the mother should have bothered. Maybe she thought that a civil ceremony had made it more certain that the younger man would stay with her, even when the illness she suffered ravaged her appearance as she neared the end of her life.

At the time of David's meeting with her, she had seemed in sufficient remission for him to have talked about her daughter and questioned her, gently, about her new husband.

'He was all she could have wished for, according to her,' was how David put it. 'Thoughtful, considerate and amusing, she said. They had met when he was holidaying on the island the previous winter, when he had fallen in with some of her old friends in a bar at one of the more swanky hotels.

She had already begun to be something of an invalid, so welcomed the attentions of the young man. She said that, rather than beach and clubs, he preferred to sit with her on her veranda. Mind you, it's massive and shaded, overlooking the sea. She has a bed made up there and it's where I interviewed her. She offered me some good rum, something I've never taken to, but hers was great. And the cocktails on the island - well...!'

He looked satisfied, if not downright smug.

David then recounted how Mrs Anderson had written to McShea after he left at the end of his holiday, persuading him to move in with her in her manorial home in Norfolk over the summer. The French home was rarely used. In the UK they had spent their days going for gentle walks in the countryside and entertaining some of the neighbours. Her health was not improving, and her doctor had advised her not to return to Barbados. But she was adamant that the climate was good for her, and her spacious bungalow allowed all the fresh air through its many verandas that she could desire.

David described how the building was as open as possible to the breezes that blew off the sea, modifying the heat of the sun, and the sea air smelt fresh and health-giving. So the two travelled together in September, and he took over as master of the house.

The household consisted of a husband and wife team, the maid, Suzanna, and Albert, the driver/gardener, with a cook employed during the winter season. McShea could transfer his work, as a graphic artist designing websites, anywhere in the world where there is wifi, but since he had moved in, he had had neither time nor need to do much paid work. He was being kept in quite a luxurious style.

David was less impressed with the younger Adonis than was the doting invalid. He found McShea, he said, superficially attractive, with dark Celtic features, but under the flamboyance and jollity he discerned a calculating mind and an edge of hardness. Ivor McShea ('call me Mack') was one of those self-centred people who appears to be all attentiveness and affability, but on whom you would not want to turn your back. Cynical, my David.

David asked him for his laptop, tablet and smartphone and anything else that could reveal information. But, and this is what made David's suspicious mind go into overdrive, McShea had bought a brand new laptop in London just before returning, destroying the old hard drive and recycling the casing.

Having had his smartphone stolen while on the Tube, he had cancelled his mobile contract and now just used a cheap Pay-as-you-go around the island.

'But you work in website design!' protested David.

'Yes, but I transferred all the important data onto the new laptop and anyway, shan't be doing much of that while I have a wife to tend to. Incidentally,' he chided, jovially, 'you addressed my wife as Mrs Anderson. She is not that anymore. Mrs McShea now, if you please!'

David reported all that with a tone that suggested less than respect for the new husband. I thought he was being a little judgmental, as there sounded perfectly good reasons why someone would want to start a new life with a new laptop. However, if McShea is a suspect for the murder of Sophie, this causing all traces of possible contact with her to be stolen or destroyed did him no favours. David began to put extradition plans in place, preferring to have him interviewed by professionals in the UK.

But my money was on the piano teacher. And shortly after, we received a bombshell on that score.

Chapter 13

Sunday

THE NEXT DAY BROKE too early. We are normally up by seven a.m. if we intend going to the 8.30 Mass, but five o'clock is too early for anyone.

Except the police. The Norfolk police had really important news. Smith-Humphries had been found.

Dead.

He had apparently drowned himself in one of the Broads, east of Norwich.

'How do you know it was suicide?' asked David reasonably, sitting up suddenly. He clutched the cordless phone handset in his right hand and banged on the pillow to wake me with his left. I had partly wakened at the ringtone, but now was fully awake. 'Yes, yes, I see'. It is maddening when you can hear only half of a conversation. 'Let me know. I'll be with you as soon as possible. Thanks.'

He turned to me.

'Right. I'm off to Norfolk. Smith-Humphries was found late last night in one of the Broads. His car had been spotted hidden in an unused lane near to the water. They dredged the part of the lake nearest the lane and found him, weighted with rocks in his pockets and in a bag around his neck, under the water. He is having a post mortem this morning and they'll confirm when he went in, but they think it was some weeks ago. His laptop was found in the car and I'm going to recover it and see what it says. It could be really decisive in the hunt for Sophie's killer. We may have him!'

Suppressing a wish to go with him as a break from London for the day, I watched him dress and shave and waved him off. He was picking up Frances White, his Sergeant who is a capable if unattractive woman of my age. I felt no jealousy when David and she were working together as I knew that she was not his type. She had dull mousy hair and a podgy face with a poor complexion. Poor girl, I doubt she ever had much fun socially. She was hardworking and wanted promotion up the ladder more than anything, but her lack of imagination would be a drawback. It is one thing to be able to carry out other people's orders, but quite another to be able to foresee situations and problems. I imagine her interviewing technique to be thorough and dull, extracting lots of minor information but not the crucial slip or hint that could take the line of questioning to a successful climax.

However, David and she work well together and she looks up to him with admiration, maybe even something more.

They were gone for the whole day, and both returned about ten at night. I made him and Frances a mug of tea and we chatted about this and that until David drove her home.

Helena and I waited anxiously for news of the investigation, as neither of us had let on to Frances that we knew anything about it. When David finally returned, I thrust in his hand a glass of his favourite malt whisky and let him explain the day's events.

There was evidence on the laptop, confirmed by the postmortem, that pointed to the suicide having taken place on the Monday of the last week of October, five days before the murder of Sophie.

There was also what amounted to a confession of long-term child abuse. He had stopped the activity some years earlier at a time when similar cases where making headlines.

As we suspected, Smith-Humphries had been blackmailed. The social media messages by the troll were a result of his not having complied with the demands of the blackmailer. He had not enough money to pay, and had not realized the power of Internet tweeting going viral.

When he found the alterations to his website and the messages, he knew that his life would not be worth living – social disgrace, lack of livelihood and even prison all loomed. He decided on drowning as a way of ending his life.

Unfortunately for the investigation, neither Smith-Humphries nor his tormentor mentioned any names. Nor could the technical experts track the source of the messages. The blackmailer-cum-troller had to be someone both very devious and very experienced in information technology. A music student hardly fitted that description, so the link with Sophie was very tenuous. If she had been the subject of abuse herself, we would never know.

I asked if anything had been found of interest on Sophie's laptop, which had been in police possession for several weeks. According to David, the only useful information drawn from it was the identity of the anonymous famous musician with whom she had had an affair. Sophie had left clues, as she had researched her quarry thoroughly before, presumably, effecting an introduction.

The evidence pointed to Rainer Hoffman, a celebrity pianist in his forties. David and I googled him together. In my opinion, shared I would guess by most of the women in the world, he was totally handsome, with thick wavy slightly greying hair, a chiselled chin covered in designer stubble, and a perma-tan. Even David agreed he has a certain something. Hoffman actually deserves his celebrity, it seems, as the critics consider him the foremost virtuoso of our day, not just a pretty face. Unusually for a classical musician, his is a household name, touring the world giving recitals in all the capital cities.

He has a wife in Florida and half a dozen children, some their own and others adopted, being disabled or otherwise 'hard to place'. That contributed to his reputation as a doting family man and generous philanthropist. A hero in the media, with a massive fan following. Lucky Sophie, maybe.

The last time he was in London was in the late Autumn, the end of October to the beginning of November, and he was due to return within the next few days for a nationwide tour, beginning with a concert at the Royal Albert Hall. David had already made arrangements to interview him and had filed the paperwork for authorization to confiscate his smartphone, tablet and anything else electronic he brings with him. At the height of his career, Hoffman would have a lot to lose. Indulging in a clandestine affaire with a young music student would not enhance his reputation. In fact, it could ruin him, utterly.

'It is too soon to jump to conclusions,' David said with maddening reasonableness. He detected my growing suspicions just from my widening eyes as we discovered more about the musician. That is what makes him a good detective. He reads body language proficiently. 'Let's see when he comes and we'll get more info.'

On the other hand, David tends not to read books all the way through, so it's fairly safe for me to unload at this point...

So far I have probably given the impression that everything in our marriage was tickety-boo, as Bertie Wooster might have said... Well, I dare say it is – compared with many others. But. There is a but, and it may be all my own fault.

Somehow I thought that being married would be better, more satisfying, more life-completing. It may simply be that I am too different from David, that I want something more than he is able to provide. By that I do not intend to demean him. It is not his fault. He is happy with what he is, what I am, what we have together. He does not have this yearning that I am cursed with. For him, life does not get much better than having somewhere decent to live, a steady and interesting job and a wife with whom he gets on and enjoys having sex with.

My problem, one of them, is that this is not enough. I don't what would be, exactly. It is just that I was expecting more from what a relationship could bring. I was brought up by Nana Ivy to think that men were sensitive to women's manners and feelings. She taught me how to sit and dress modestly; not to mention bodily functions; not to laugh too loud, and, worst of all, not to appear to know more than the man does.

She is as much of a romantic as I am, and probably for the same reason. In her case, to escape from a poverty that afflicts both body and mind, and in mine to forget that I was rejected by my mother. We have both steeped our imagination in novels from the eighteenth and nineteenth centuries. Their writers projected their dreams and fantasies into their novels, knowing that so many women wanted them to be true. We want the men in our lives to be sensitive, yet strong; deep and emotional, yet in control of their feelings and able to verbalize them with easy fluency. Nana Ivy's husband, whom I barely knew, was a gentle man of little education but not lacking in intelligence. His problem was that he did not have the vocabulary to express his thoughts and feelings in words, so that Nana Ivy spent long hours talking with me, sharing all her thoughts with her granddaughter rather than her husband. Her heroes were the poets, men who could shape ideas in a language that carried meaning and sounded mellifluous. Mine were the women who created imaginative worlds where men were either dastardly or of superior sensitivity. How I longed to spend my days in the book-lined study or library of a scholarly, handsome, gentle and wise man. We would go on cultural tours and learn to sing and play instruments together and laugh at the wit of amusing companions.

So, poor David. He is never going to be the heroic character in my silly immature fantasies, just as I will never be a contented wife prepared to settle for the hum-drum while there is so much world out there to be experienced. As they say in the Bronx: 'Enough, already'.

Chapter 14

Monday

THE NEXT MORNING I turned in to work to face my desk-top covered in paperwork, and it took several hours just to work through half of it. Lunch in the cafeteria, then on to a play-reading of *The Witlings*.

There had been other readings, and a few cast changes, but this was the first I had been able to attend.

Michael was in good form, joking with the cast and deferring to Dorothy with admirable respect. There was a discussion of how wearing costume would make a difference and Michael agreed to arrange for items of costume and small props to be borrowed from the Victoria and Albert, where he had contacts.

He made a call on his mobile and announced that a large box would be available for collection the next day. I volunteered to pick that up later on the following morning as I would be taking the car to St John's Wood and could go on easily to Knightsbridge from there.

An old friend of Nana Ivy had recently been taken to the St John and St Elizabeth hospital in St John's Wood and I had promised Nana on the telephone that I would call in to visit her, and Tuesday morning was a good time to do so, as my diary was freer then than at other times.

The rest of the rehearsal went well, with much laughter, provoked both by the script and by Michael's witty comments to encourage his young team. He got the best out of people through humour, even when criticizing them, enabling them to admit their mistakes while smiling.

I went from fun to boredom, having to attend a compulsory meeting for all college staff, taken department by department, about awareness training for issues concerning one minority group or another. There was nothing that I had not heard a thousand times, so sat doodling, and musing on the case of Sophie's murder. Suddenly, my name was mentioned.

'Well, Dr Deane', I heard through a mist ('Julia!' hissed a friend sitting next to me) 'and what would you do if you were confronted with a student making an inappropriate comment on another student's body shape?'

'Er, I'd caution him .... or her.....and I'd, um, repeat the college's code of non-discriminatory behaviour.'

Phew, that seemed acceptable and I sank a bit lower in my chair, waiting impatiently for the end of the session. Afterwards, my friendly neighbour and another colleague invited me for a coffee and chat. After that welcome break I saw a student who was late with an essay and, having scooped up some paperwork into my briefcase, left for home.

That evening Helena was out to the cinema with her new friend from downstairs, and David and I had the flat to ourselves. I cooked, and he washed. Then we sat on the sofa, not yet transformed into Helena's bed, and instead of watching television, talked about holidays, and what we would be doing for Christmas.

I get annoyed with the provisional nature of police leave, which can be cancelled at a moment's notice. It means that holidays are never guaranteed and I can never be sure that David will be home over major religious festivals. One drawback is that people always have to come to us, so that I am not left to travel alone.

We discussed the options, as Helena seemed to be in no hurry to return to the commune. Usually, Nana Ivy comes up to us and sleeps on the living-room sofa-bed, which was Helena's territory now, and David's parents take over our bedroom. David and I move into the house of one of our friends from church. Jane lives nearby in Wordsworth Place, a small gated development of town houses and a block of flats for retired people, built twenty years ago in what had been the car park of St Dominic's Priory.

We often meet her on a Sunday morning, as she is a regular reader at the 8.30 Mass. She invites us and a few others round to her house for coffee afterwards. A former teacher in her sixties, Jane has parents still living and she goes to stay with them over Christmas, giving up her house for us to sleep in.

Jane is one of life's driving forces, ever seeking new interests and activities, although highly gifted in all aspects of needlework. Not in robust health, yet she has the mind of a youngster, keeping up with trends and fashions and even fluent in 'youth speak', though lacking children of her own. She haunts the trendy Camden High Street, market and canal lock area, picking up bargain clothes and ideas and making lots of friends among the market stall holders.

She lacks a car but has a parking space, so kindly lent me the remote control for the gates to Wordsworth Place, and at times when there is no vacant space in front of my house, I use hers. In exchange, I run her to airports or to her parents or to hospital visits when she needs them and if I am free.

Mr Hobson in our downstairs flat has no car either, so David and I have the luxury of two nose-to-kerb spaces for our cars just in front of our house.

This year Christmas plans are complicated with having Helena on the sofa. Not inviting Nana Ivy is unthinkable, and yet Jane has only one room used for sleeping. The boxroom in her little house is taken up with a sewing machine, a dress-maker's dummy and racks of clothes. Open shelves line the walls, filled with lengths of material of every type and colour, and two large rush baskets overflow with enough haberdashery to open a shop. She is an avid dressmaker and provides a couple of local boutiques with the occasional high-end made-to-measure outfit.

She also adapts historic costumes for the stage, and I needed to talk to her about our Burney production and to arrange dates for fitting our stock of eighteenth-century dresses onto the figures of our cast members. She would love the challenge.

David had brought home some brochures from travel companies, and seemed keen to return to Barbados, this time for pleasure. He shone with delight at the thought of our taking a spring break of a week, lying on the beach, scuba diving or jet skiing around St Peter's Bay.

'If we went in April,' he enthused, 'we could catch the Reggae Festival. What about it?'

'OK,' I admitted. 'It sounds fun. Let's go for it. But you do the arranging, for once.'

We did not realise then just how much we would need a holiday after the terrible events that were to unfold.

Chapter 15

Tuesday

THE NEXT MORNING I took the car and drove west to St John's Wood. I spent a frustrating few minutes in the car park of the John and Lizzie's looking fruitlessly for spaces, then parked in a nearby street and fed the meter. I went in to see Nana Ivy's friend and sat with her for a quarter of an hour. There was no point in staying longer as she was too confused to grasp who I was, addressing me as 'Doreen' for some reason. She could not remember Ivy Jackson, although they had known each other for two thirds of a century, although rallied a little when I mentioned my grandmother's maiden name.

'Oh, Ivy York, why didn't you say? How is Ivy? And her young man, whatsisname? Works with cranes on the docks. Has he proposed to her yet?'

Wherever she was, it was not here. I left her to it and wondered how I would break the news to Nana that her friend was no longer in the same world as the rest of us. I was musing on the nature of youth and friendship, and that led me to think about Toyah. I got to the car, and with plenty of time on the meter, and considered giving her a call to see how she was. I also wanted to let her know to tell her friend Laura about Smith-Humphries and what had happened to her childhood molester. I got through to Toyah almost immediately.

'Hi, Dr Deane, Julia, good to hear you!'

'Where are you? What's all the noise?'

'I'm just leaving Broadway tube station. On my way to pick something up from the house.'

'But you can't! It's off bounds. Nobody can get in there. The police are guarding it!'

I was worried. This was not a good move. I knew that Toyah could physically get into the house, but the police had forbidden entry to it until all danger from the intruder had passed.

'Oh, I'll only be a minute. There's a book I left there that I really need, and I want to check that my harpsichord is still OK. Don't worry!'

'Hold on, I'm coming. I'll see you there. Wait outside , and I'll go in with you. No, wait down the road, by the bus stop. I'll see you there as soon as can. I'm in St John's Wood right now, so it'll take a few minutes.'

I drove through the streets of London as quickly as the traffic and speed limits would allow, and arrived in Fulham feeling anxious and annoyed. I wished Toyah had not decided to ignore police advice, or had arranged for someone to be with her. I looked out for the young woman at the bus stop, but there was nobody there. Nor was she waiting in the street.

I intended parking just in front of the house, but as usual all the parking permit places were taken and I had to turn into the side road and park up there. I scurried round to the front door as fast as I could, but found it locked. So I pushed open the side gate and walked around the back of the semi. The back door was closed but unlocked, so I went in and called for Toyah.

No answer.

By now I was in the kitchen and chucked my shoulder bag on the table, fumbling in it for my mobile, and then called Toyah. Fortunately I had her on speed dial.

In a moment, somewhere near me, there was a suppressed tinkle of a harpsichord ringtone. Her phone! I followed the sound into the hallway and saw her coat slung over the end of the banister, from the pocket of which the sound was coming, louder and louder. I pulled the phone from the pocket, cancelled the call and the sound stopped.   Oh my God.

'Toyah!' I shouted really loudly. Still nothing. The next call was with trembling hands to David. I hurriedly garbled where I was and that Toyah was not here.

'Get out. Go home. Call me…and don't touch anything!'

I obeyed my husband without a moment's thought. There's a first time for everything.   Turning, I dropped my phone into my pocket, and hurried back through the kitchen, pausing only to throw my bag over my shoulder. I threw open the back door and slammed it shut behind me. I was round the house, through the side gate and down the front path as fast as I could go. Then turning right, I took off at a run along the pavement, round the corner into the side street and made it to the car, my fingers already enfolding the electronic key in my coat pocket. Then, suddenly, a tall figure loomed behind me. I heard a thwack and was aware of a sharp blinding pain at the back of my head. My vision clouded, the whiteness of my car swirling before me and fast approaching my face. Then total darkness.

I came to, muzzily, and feeling close to vomiting, in a grey shadowy space I took to be some sort of large garage or storage room. I began to focus at the same time as becoming aware of being unable to move about. I was tied to a chair, one of those coloured plastic stacking things, by a cord around my thighs and waist secured around the tops of the chair legs. My wrists were tied together behind my back and some kind of filthy cloth stuffed into my mouth, which was bound with duct tape.

The room I was held in was large, the size of two or three garages, and poorly lit by one low-amp bulb dangling from a central wire. I could see by turning my head that I was not alone. There was another figure slumped and tied in another chair like mine.

A young woman, unconscious, was almost doubled over. Her long hair fell over her knees. Toyah! It took a moment to recognize her, which I could only do by the clothes and hair. I grunted my alarm in the hope that she might hear and sit up. I began to panic as breathing proved difficult through just my nose and tried to calm myself down into taking slow, deep, breaths.

Thinking was difficult, panicking so much more natural just then. Then the pain kicked in. Not just at the back of my head, but the front too. My forehead must have hit the car as I fell and blood had poured from an open wound down over my right eye. It was still sticky and made opening and seeing through that eye difficult.

I was just trying to look down at myself to see if I could see blood on my coat, when two things happened at once.

I noticed that I was not wearing my coat, and involuntarily shivered violently, partly from cold and partly from shock.

The other was the arrival of two men. As they opened the door, I caught a glimpse of empty shelves in the better lit room they were coming from. Not only shelves along the wall, there were also rows of shelving inside the room – an empty shop. A small supermarket, such as a Spar store.

The two men looked at us, and then answered a call from a third man inside the store and returned, shutting the door behind them and leaving us again in deep gloom.   As my one good eye adjusted to the poor light I noticed a clutter of empty cardboard cartons piled loosely on each other along the base of one wall. A Health and Safety notice, a scribbled-on holiday and duty rota chart, and a calendar of uncertain date with a picture of a grinning topless model decorated the wall that I could see. Cobwebs and dirt joined the discarded cigarette stubs and squashed-in beer cans.

There must have been an outer door behind me, as the room was momentarily lit as another person entered. A big man with a lumberjack hat. He barely paused to notice Toyah and me as he passed by and through the inner door to the shop. Seconds later, three men entered from the shop.

One went to Toyah and two towards me. The one by Toyah took her hair in his hands and pulled up her head. I could see that she was not gagged, but unconscious. She began to come to and the man dropped her hair and put his hand over her mouth instead. Her eyes half opened, as she struggled into full consciousness, and then widened with alarm and terror. The men by me watched this, then turned to me and one of them yanked off the duct tape with, it felt like, several layers of facial skin. As he removed the cloth from inside my mouth and I gulped in air like a drowning man, the other snarled in a heavily accented rasping voice,

'Don't make a sound!'

Then he growled, 'Where is it? Don't play about with us. Just tell us where it is, and we'll let you go.'

My confusion was genuine.

'What? What do you want? Where is what?'

'The cello, of course. The fancy cello, the old one. The one your friend would not sell us.'

'I haven't a clue! D'you mean Sophie Anderson's?'

'Of course, bitch!'

He and the man the other side of me spoke a few words to each other in some East European tongue, Russian or Polish, I was not in a position to analyse it just then. Then they both bent close, so close I could smell their tobacco-laden breath. The first repeated his idiotic question. Again I denied knowing anything about it.

As they straightened up, I realized that they may not have known that Sophie was dead.

They said something to the man gagging Toyah with his hand. He brought a knife out of his pocket, released her mouth but placed the blade against her throat, taking her hair again with his free hand so preventing her any movement. Her eyes and anguished expression told me all.

'See your friend?' said my interrogator with the rasping voice. 'She will get it if you don't tell us.'

Just then the man with the lumberjack hat entered from the shop, leaving the door open and allowing a little more light into our store room.

'Ah!' he exclaimed with sudden recognition. 'Is thees the beetch who stung my eyes? Give it to her!'

With that, one of the men slapped me hard across the face with the base of his palm. My cheek burned and then stung and my brain seemed to rattle against the skull. It took some moments for the world to stop revolving. My one good eye welled up with unwanted tears preventing my seeing anything at all. A few moments later and anger took over. I shouted at them.

'Don't you know she's dead! Don't you know whoever killed her has the bloody thing?'

Silence. Then raised voices as the four men all spoke together, arguing and shouting at each other. Then one turned to me, I still could not see properly, but it sounded like the man with the hat,

'Vee know she dead. But ze cello... ?'

'It's not here, not with us. Never was. You thought it was in the house, but it wasn't. She had it with her when she was murdered. She was found, but not the cello. Nor her coat. Now let us go!'

More shouting in Russian. It occurred to me, with a lurching stomach-feeling, that while we were thought to have knowledge of what they wanted, they needed us alive. But now....

Just as my mind was awash with apprehension, both the outer door behind me and the shop front door before me crashed open. Black helmeted figures burst through with guns primed and aimed, and repeating deafening shouts of 'Police! Put down your weapons!'

Relief and exhilaration mixed with terror as more and more armed men seemed to fill the store room. With looks of weary defeat, our captors raised their hands.

'Put down your weapons!'

Then a percussion of clatter, clatter, clatter as guns and knives hit the concrete floor.

David and other plain clothed and uniformed men entered through the shop door. David at once knelt at my feet, trying with desperate fumblings to untie the knots in the cords binding me. He stretched out his right hand and someone placed one of the surrendered knives into it, with which he sawed at a cord until it came apart.

He then pulled me out of the chair, emotionally clasping me to himself with relief. Another officer untied the cord around my hands and, feeling them free, I flung them around David's body, drawing him ever closer and sobbing uncontrollably.

My sobbing stopped abruptly as I remembered Toyah. I turned to see her being comforted by a uniformed policewoman, just one of the crowd of law enforcers within the storeroom.

Others were handcuffing the thugs and leading them out. Toyah and I then drew away from our comforters and towards each other, embracing and sobbing afresh.

Eventually, when the police had withdrawn, leaving just David and us, we were shepherded outside and accompanied to a car. We two women sat in the back, holding hands, while David sat in front and a uniformed sergeant drove us to the nearest Accident and Emergency unit to be checked out.

We were medically examined and my forehead gash sewn and taped up. As we had both been concussed, our heads were x-rayed and scanned, and we were kept in overnight as a precaution, in adjacent beds in a four-bed ward.

Fed and sedated, with David in attendance, I slept soundly but woke feeling wretched, with a blinding headache and half-closed eyes. The sight in the mirror that I had asked David to hold up was appalling! A creature with swollen, black eyes, a bruised and raw scar and highly reddened cheeks looked back at me.

I looked over to Toyah, still sleeping, and noticed with relief that she had suffered less facial damage. David smiled indulgently, and assured me I was still beautiful to him. His words failed to comfort, but I appreciated the thought behind them.

He told me that he had been in touch with the squad deputed to deal with this incident, and had learned some interesting facts. The Eastern European thugs were, they admitted, employed by the Russian oligarch. He was still in his home country, but had commissioned them to acquire the rare and expensive baroque cello that Sophie's mother had bought her. This boss had not given explicit orders, but had just told them to get hold of it in any way they could.

David assured me that the gang would 'have the book thrown at them'. They faced years in prison, followed by deportation. Meanwhile the legal team was working at seeing if there was some way in which the Russian could face prosecution. Extradition from Russia of one of President Putin's friends would not be an easy matter, and the Home Office would have had to be involved.

As Sophie had the cello with her when she was murdered, the Russian, and his side-kicks, were ruled out from the list of suspects for her murder – unless she had passed the bulky instrument to another person before meeting her murderer, but that seemed unlikely. Nobody had come forward with that information. Nor could she have stashed it in one of the college's lockers, as they had all been checked previously by the investigation team.

I stayed dozing in bed for a couple of hours, feeling my head was splitting apart and as if my face had been sat on by a particularly heavy elephant. By mid morning, Toyah had wakened and seemed reasonably cheerful.

We were visited by a consultant who asked about our heads and general wellbeing. He felt the bumps on the backs of our heads and watched us stand and walk a few steps, then pronounced us fit to go home.

David gathered the two of us as if we were poorly sheep, and took us to wait for him in the lobby, while he brought his car round to be as near to the door as was allowed.

As we drove towards home, I asked Toyah how she felt about returning to her room in the hall of residence.

'OK,' she said. 'But I think I'll just stay in for a few days. I'll be able to move back in to the house now they've caught the intruder, won't I? My lease does not run out till the end of the year, and I've got so many things there.'

David agreed that that should be all right, but he would check with the crime team first.

Meanwhile, Toyah was to spend the rest of the day, at least, with us, being cosseted and fed. An ordeal such as she and I had gone through would take some time to get over.

David was torn between wanting to stay with us and being keen to watch the interrogation of the thugs who had walloped us. He was not allowed to take part in that investigation, being personally close to the victims. He had even had to argue his case to continue to pursue the murder inquiry. Friendship with Toyah did not, it was agreed by the top brass, compromise the investigation into her house-mate's death, and might even allow a clue to be discovered through conversations.

My mother caused the biggest shock when we got into the flat. She was consideration itself!

Chapter 16

I THREW OFF MY CLOTHES, donned my thickest nightdress – this was no time for Ann Summers negligée – and crawled into my half of the bed. Toyah stripped to her underclothes and was put into David's side of the marital bed, where she promptly turned onto her side and fell asleep. I propped pillows up behind my back and pulled the duvet to my neck, dozing and then waking, and wished I hadn't.

I had flashbacks either sleeping or waking; seeing faces of malevolence, wondering how people could be so unfeeling, so cruel to other human beings. But I knew it was nothing compared with what women, men and even children went through in war zones. I thought how close I had been to dying, and wondered whether my faith would stand up to the reality of knowing my last moment had arrived.

Fortunately I had been spared that last terrifying awareness of mortality. Should it have been so frightening? Was I not a believer in an afterlife of supreme and unimaginable bliss? Somehow that did not seem such a cast-iron reality. Why was I doubting? Maybe it is natural after a traumatic event, and yet where is the belief that sailors are supposed to exhibit in storms, or soldiers on the battlefield? How was it that I could entertain doubts when I had been so faithful until then? I found I was chiding myself for my lack of trust, remembering that real faith is not simply assent to doctrinal statements, credal affirmations, but a willingness to lean on God. I had to let go of my questions – the 'how can it be?' niggles – and simply admit that my knowledge, all knowledge, is finite.

I remembered a comforting story I found once in a parish bulletin (I since learnt that it was by Walter Dudley Cavert), about some grubs that lived at the bottom of an old pond. They wondered why none of their group ever returned after crawling up the stem of a plant to the top of the water. They promised each other that whoever went up next would return to tell the others all about it. When one of them felt the urge to seek the surface he went and was wonderfully transformed, becoming a dragonfly with beautiful wings. As he flew over the pond he knew that, even if he were able to return, none of the others would recognise him as one of their own.

We are like babies in the womb who consider that life in that place must be all that there is. So we too think we know all there is to be known, and yet how little do we truly understand.

With thoughts like these I tried hard to console myself and find relief, although I would shudder involuntarily whenever something reminded me of that dreadful shop storeroom. Usually it was a pain, in my head or wrists or elsewhere. The gloomy thoughts were to recur intermittently for days and even weeks.

David rang my head of department to tell him what had happened and with apparent concern he suggested that I just take the rest of the week off, as he would find cover for me, or cancel my seminars and tutorials. There was no way I was going to appear in public until my face had returned to normal. Black, puffy eyes, large scar with white tapes across it, and brightly reddened cheeks are not what I wanted to show to the world. In fact I was feeling so shaken and tired, all I wanted to do was sleep for weeks, or hug David, or cry into my pillow. Now don't say 'What a wimp' until it has happened to you. God forbid.

I remembered my offer to Tom, to take him to Chawton House to hear Dr Augustus Oakwood, but my call went straight to his voicemail. I left the message that I would not be going, but that he should find his own way there, if he could. Perhaps Oakwood would take him; it would be worth asking.

My disappointment at not going back to Chawton House caused me to feel real anger at the thugs who had prevented me. What a contrast the house presented from the dingy storeroom. Chawton House drew me to it as few others could, knowing that within it was a rich treasury of first editions, manuscripts and hard-to-find books of the writings of women. Here was hard evidence of the ability of some privileged women to express themselves in public at a time of crippling male hegemony. Here were memories, in writing and print, of what some fortunate women were thinking and dreaming. Thoughts and dreams otherwise lost to us – as are those of women throughout the world today who have no access to education or a public forum. I lay there, victim of male macho bullies, working myself up into a throbbing, furious feminism.

David could not have been sweeter. Kindness itself. However, even he got on my nerves a bit. I was not comfortable lying, sitting, sleeping, waking. Plus I felt embarrassed that my face resembled a boxer's after ten rounds in the ring.

David was keen to return to work. After a hurried lunch, he came in to kiss me goodbye, commiserate, and promise to 'slam the bastards up' for what they had done to us. Toyah came to in the afternoon and felt much refreshed. I admired her resilience and felt ashamed at my own self-indulgent introspections. She went to the bathroom for a shower and afterwards relaxed on the sofa in the living room, flipping through unread newspapers and supplements from the weekend.

Helena fussed around us as she had never done before – bringing us cups of tea and asking what more she could do. Several times I tried to get up and get on, but the effort was too much, and each time I sank back onto the pillows at my back, propping me up, and dozed and slept. By evening, I felt up to watching a little television, and joined Toyah in a light supper, each with a glass of wine and a bowl of soup on a tray, all lovingly prepared and brought to us by my doting mother.

When David returned at about seven o'clock, he took Toyah home to her room in the hall of residence. She promised to keep in close touch and to ring the hospital should her headache worsen or any other ailment bother her. Her move back into the house she had once shared with others could take place whenever she felt ready to go, but David advised her to stay at the Hall, with people around her, for the next few days.

Chapter 17

THE NEXT MORNING, alone in the flat with Helena, she and I got into a deep discussion about the paths our lives had taken. I shared with her, for the first time ever, my sense of abandonment by the person I would have thought loved me the most. I told her how resentful I was in my teens, and how Nana Ivy would speak up for her, while no doubt feeling as bitter as I did.

'Well, love,' she said, gently, almost tearfully. 'There was a reason you know.'

'Yes, you didn't want me talking in Welsh!'

'It wasn't just that. There were other reasons too. I didn't want to go into them with you before...'

'Go on. You can now.'

'Well, you know there were eight of us when we started. Some left, one died, others came. Well, one of the men – not your father, not Tim – said how young girls turned him on and how he couldn't wait until you and the other children born on the farm were nine or ten. He said they were the best years for sex. Well, you see...'

I did, feeling rather sick. Not another. Was not Smith-Humphries enough?

'Why didn't you tell me before? Why leave me to think you rejected me? Why not tell Nana Ivy?'

'Because she would have made me leave, that's why. He's not a bad man, Graham, not really. Just has this weakness. I don't think he's ever done anything about it, but he does like looking at pictures of children with nothing on.'

'O God, mother! You must report him! You can't risk letting him abuse any child around!'

'Well, there aren't any. All the mothers sent their children away. Broke our hearts it did. Mind you, Tim can't stand children, so it was probably for the best. You can't live in a commune with babies crying all around. He can get quite angry if he's kept awake.'

Oh, she is incorrigible. She still preferred her chosen way of life with the odd-balls on a muddy draughty farm in the middle of nowhere to bringing up her own child.

By the afternoon I was ready for some reading, and settled down with a book in my dressing gown, legs up on the sofa and under a rug.

By the Friday I was able to do some real work – writing reports, assessing essays and writing up notes for my next few lectures. An important public lecture was scheduled for the last week of term, but I was not sure that I would be ready to give it.

I knew what I was going to talk about – the nature of musical performance as described in Fanny Burney's novels, with excerpts from her journals and letters as further illustration. I could almost give the talk straight away, without notes, but needed to ensure the progression of ideas was orderly and all references accounted for.

But would my face be reasonable by then and my system sufficiently recovered? At least I would act as if they would be, so that I could take the stand, fully prepared, if they were. I had about ten days to prepare for it, and then remembered, with the sickening premonition that I would not have time to do it, the work needed to prepare for the examinations that confronted undergrads as soon as they returned after the Christmas vacation.

Sometimes I felt that I was in a race where the finishing line was always being moved further away, like the famous badger-moving goal-posts.

When taking up this work, I had foolishly imagined myself methodically preparing and delivering lectures and basking in the admiration of inspired students as they plunged ever deeper and with ever increasing enthusiasm into the subject of the literature of yesteryear.

Instead, most time seemed to be taken up with administration tasks that at one time specially trained people undertook; preparing and attending meetings; assessing students and their work in the particular and peculiar jargon of modern education; and preparing examinations. All this while being expected to publish numerous articles and write deep and groundbreaking books that gain media attention and attract hordes of students to our particular place of learning. I have had this rant before. And no doubt shall do again.

I started working early the next day, Saturday, feeling much more recovered and guilty that I had allowed time to pass with little to show for it. Helena went off to buy the shopping on the list I drew up for her, and I sat at the kitchen table tapping away at my laptop.

I was jarred out of my absorption with the work by a call on my mobile. Dr Oakwood, bless him, was enquiring after my health as he had heard about my ordeal from the Chawton people.

'You didn't make it last night? I hear you were hoping to, but I guess with your trouble you couldn't face it, right?'

'Absolutely. I had so wanted to hear you. How did it go?'

'Fine, fine. The folk here seemed to like it. Great place, isn't it! I had no idea – but intend to come back pretty often. It's got so much.'

'Indeed it has.' (Why do I go all Jane Austeny when talking to Americans?)

'Say, shame Tom didn't show up either. He was really eager to come, last time I heard from him. Mind you, he didn't show at a meeting I arranged with him earlier this week, either. Do you know how he is? Last I knew he was going to head off to Austria in the new year, to where I found the Haydn.'

'Oh, dear. No. I haven't heard from him for ages. I left a message with him about last night, but he didn't return my call. I hope he's all right. I don't really know much about him, who his friends are, or anything, so can't really ask anyone. I'll try him again.'

'Do. And let him know I'm happy to go over anything with him about how I found the material, and all that. Tell him to get in touch as soon as he can. I may be popping home for a few days over the vacation, so he needs to see me soon. Say, while we're on it. How about I take you out to dinner next week, so we can talk about Dr Burney and I can fill you in with what I said last night?'

'Fantastic. Thanks very much. I'd love it. How about Tuesday, that's a good time for me?'

'Tuesday's fine then. Great. I'll pick you up from your college at about, what? Seven?'

Oh, a date! I had not had one of those since before I met David. This date there'll be no smooching and fumbling with bra straps or any of that, just civilized conversation between academics. How I'm getting old!

David was fine about it when he got in from work. Even happy that I was back in the land of the living, as he called it. He asked after Toyah, and I felt suddenly guilty that I had not spoken to her since she had left us on Wednesday.

I called her up and she sounded as bright as ever. No lasting harm then. Thank goodness. We discussed what we had been doing and she asked if I could help her move back in her house on Monday. I happily agreed, noting that I had an afternoon free from engagements, and was already a little bored with working non-stop.

Chapter 18

ON MONDAY LUNCHTIME I took the Tube home, picked up the car, and made for Toyah's hall of residence. She met me with all her things ready, and we packed the car and drove over to Fulham. I parked in the usual side street, looking left and right a little nervously, and helped carry her things round the corner and into her house.

Everything was as we left it, although there were some traces of black sooty residue around items of door furniture and light fittings, where dusting for fingerprints had taken place.

Toyah dumped her things in her room while I made a cup of tea for each of us, without milk as there was none in the refrigerator.

After liquid refreshment, she announced,

'Let's cheer ourselves up by going shopping!'

Great idea. 'Let me introduce you to the Hampstead Bazaar shop in St Christopher's Place, just off Oxford Street, ' I offered.

I usually resent the time spent shopping for clothes in large department stores, but this place is different. There is always something I find I just have to buy there _ in a colour and material that is soft and simple, with a straightforward design that flatters all figures.

As we were about to leave, I noticed on the Welcome mat, a small business card which had been posted through the letterbox.

On one side it said,

Discreet Investigations
Reputable Private Detective
References provided
Marcus P. Woodhouse
Tel. 0108 449 6326
Email: mpwoodhousepi@gmail.com

On the other,

Toyah.
Please contact me a.s.a.p.

This was intriguing. We looked at each other.

Shall we? Should we? What does it mean?

I then called David, and took him out of an important meeting with his superiors. He sounded a little tetchy.

'All right. Give me the details again, or rather, text them, now. I'll call you back. Stay there.'

We took off our coats, went into the living room and lounged on chairs while waiting for the call.

'All right. He's kosher. We've used him ourselves. Find out what he wants and call me back. Don't commit yourselves to anything. Say you'll let him know.'

With acute interest, Toyah called him, putting her phone on speaker so that I could hear what was said.

'Hello. Marcus Woodhouse? this is Toyah. You asked me to call.'

'Oh, thanks. Thanks very much. Yes, that's great. Listen. I've been taken on by someone who wants to see you. Someone you may know, but who didn't know how he could reach you. No-one was prepared to give him your contact details. You've had some trouble, I believe. But really, this is not like that. He just needs to talk to you. Will you see him?'

'Just a minute,' Toyah looked at me with the question in her expression, What do I do?

'Find out who it is, and say you'll only meet them if your friend can come too.'

She nodded and asked Woodhouse the first part of that condition. The second depended on the first being met.

'Well, I shall tell you who it is on the condition you do not pass this on.'

'OK'

'It's the pianist, Rainer Hoffman. You may know of him?'

'Of course. He was playing at the Albert Hall recently!'

My eyebrows shot up my forehead. I shook my head hard, but Toyah was already saying,

The World According to Julia

'Of course I'll see him – but only if I can bring my friend along too. She's my tutor. Well, not actually my tutor, but is helping me at college. She is married to a detective.'

I was mouthing words to her that she could not read, so she muted the phone and I told her in the most adamant way that the husband would have to come too. Three of us, or none.

I was utterly intrigued and hoped with rising excitement that Woodhouse would agree.

He did. Reluctantly, and conditional upon his client accepting those terms.

Woodhouse checked with his client while we kept David up to speed. We jumped slightly when the private detective rang us back within minutes.

'All right,' he said. 'I'll meet the three of you in the lounge of the Rembrandt Hotel, Brompton Road. It's opposite a big church, the Oratory, which is next to the V& A. At four o'clock. OK?'

At five to four the three of us were striding through the roomy outer lobby of the hotel, up the few steps and through the doors separating it from the lounge. The spacious room led into a restaurant opposite these doors. One side was glass-roofed with a bar at the head. The rest of the room had several groupings of comfortable sofas and armchairs, with one half circle turned towards a cheerfully burning log fire.

A short, thin man in a smart suit stood up from his place near to the fire, and approached us. 'Toyah Howard?' he asked, directing his hand towards her for her to shake.

She then introduced first me, 'And Detective Chief Inspector David Dean'.

When the round of handshakes had been accomplished, Woodhouse spoke, quietly.

'My client would be grateful if you would accompany me to his room on the second floor. He is waiting for you there. What he has to say cannot be said in a public place'.

His head indicated the space around him, which seemed innocently uncrowded. But Hoffman was not to know that. So we all inserted ourselves into the elevator and were wooshed up to the floor on which the maestro was staying.

Woodhouse led the way and knocked on the door to number 226. It was opened by the most suave and handsome man to whom I had ever been so close. Most professional musicians tend to the bohemian look, with wild Beethovian hair that signal, 'Genius', but not matinee idol Hoffman.

He nodded to Woodhouse, who remained outside the door, while he welcomed us in with a smile, gesturing us to take a seat.

I sat next to Toyah on the sofa, while David took one of the chairs.

Before he sat down, our host asked if we should like a drink of anything.

'Whisky I can do. Tea for four I can send down for. Would you like that? Afternoon tea, perhaps? Can I tempt you?'

We declined, preferring to get on with whatever it was he wanted to tell or ask us.

'Very well.' He sat down and leant forward, forming an arch with his fingertips, and staring at the carpet.

'You see. I've been blackmailed. For months. As you probably know. Connecting me with that girl, that cellist. And I want it to stop. Before the press get hold of it. Before my wife does.'

He looked up suddenly, fixing Toyah with a glare. She was momentarily speechless. Then blurted, 'Well, it's not me!' She looked at first bewildered, then angry.

'This is a police matter. You should have come to us. On what evidence do you claim the blackmailer is Toyah? Be careful what you say,' said David in his most solemn policemanly voice.

'Because she knew. She knew about Sophie and me, that's why. Nobody else did. It has to be her.'

'Actually she didn't,' I could not help contributing this. Nor this, 'Until now!'

Hoffman looked perplexed. He blustered. 'Well, I...I ...'

David explained.

'Until our technical people retrieved Sophie's deleted emails to and from you, nobody knew who her mystery lover had been. You did a great job of keeping your identity private. You met only in hotels, and were never seen in public together. Nor did Sophie ever tell her housemates and friends who she was seeing. Even her boyfriend did not know who it was – just that someone she met had been giving her gifts, valuable gifts.'

'So..?'

'So no-one here, no-one we know of has been blackmailing you. It must be someone else. You should have come forward before now with this information. We can find out who it is and stop him, or her. But why did you not tell us about the blackmail when we interviewed you?'

'I guess I felt too stoopid, too ashamed. Also I thought that it would stop once Sophie was... No-one likes to appear to be a dupe.

It is bad enough my having had a fling with that girl – I'm sorry. She's dead, and it's all so tragic. No-one so young should have ended up that way. Forgive me, Miss.'

I had been studying him. His classically regular features; his expensively coiffed hair and the Saville Row suit and silk tie. It all made up the perfect picture of the successful man, the alpha male who could have the pick of any woman he wanted, or so he gave the impression.

I could see why Sophie went for him. And yet there was something about him which was somewhat chilling. The single-mindedness that had made him dedicate himself to perfecting his craft, his art, had left no room for anything or anyone else. I imagined his beautiful trophy wife and the innumerable adopted children all helping to market him as the model of the perfect family man and musical genius.

Yet there was a coldness, a ruthlessness there that left me wondering if he would be capable of destroying the life of the young woman he now regretted knowing. I believed he would. I think that most people are capable of terrible deeds if the rewards outweigh the risk of penalties. That is why we need laws, and religions, and social conventions – to stop us behaving like the savages we all are. Or could be, if we have all to gain by being so.

Words of contrition are easy to say. I could see that Toyah was not impressed with them either. David then went into full police mode.

'You will have to go to Paddington Road Police Station and make a full statement about this blackmailing. Do so as soon as possible. Tonight, if you can. Take your laptop or smart phone or with whatever the blackmailer makes contact with you. We'll be able to trace who it is and stop it.'

'Thank God. I'm being drained financially. And if it ever got out, my life too would be in ruins. You will keep this all away from the press, won't you?'

'We'll see what we can do,' David said with some conviction. He meant it too. For as much as he despised the culture of celebrity, he believed that even famous rogues are entitled to their privacy.

I stood up, quickly followed by Toyah and David. Hoffman proffered his hand with cold politeness, which we took turns to shake in similar manner. Then he led the way to the door, and instructed Woodhouse kindly to see us out.

Out on the pavement of Brompton Road, David and I both looked towards the Oratory, and with Toyah's assent, the three of us crossed the busy road at the lights and trouped in there. We knelt alongside each other in a pew half way down the nave. After a few minutes' silent prayer or, in Toyah's case, reflection, I placed my right hand over Toyah's and my left on David's and we sat there, simply holding hands in companionable silence, looking around the dusty statues and other baroque splendours of that church, or what we could see through the subdued lighting in that enormous edifice.

Once we felt emotionally stronger, we left and joined the crowds of commuters and tourists all hurrying to get home, or to hotel rooms, before the menacing drizzle turned into real heavy rain.

We took the District Line at South Kensington tube station, changing at Earl's Court to go to Fulham Broadway. We walked to Toyah's house in the now teeming rain and left her while we got into my car and drove the tedious miles through traffic and rain until we reached Camden.

Annoyingly no parking spaces were available outside our house, so I dropped off David and drove round to Joan's parking spot in Wordsworth Place. Without the forethought of bringing an umbrella, I walked the last few hundred yards to home, soaking wet, cold and fairly miserable. Even my head hurt.

'Can you trace the blackmailer?' I asked, once we were inside and our hands wrapped around mugs of instant soup. 'What happened to Smith-Humphries? Did you find out who was blackmailing him? Would it be the same person?'

'First question. Yes, probably. Eventually. We haven't yet been able to trace the paedophile piano teacher's nemesis. Whoever it was is a real expert on computers. He's always one step ahead of our experts. They don't know how he does it. And possibly it is the same person, although there is little to connect them, other than one taught the child Sophie and other screwed the slightly older one. Oh, and they both played the piano.'

We left it at that and attended to our physical needs – for food, relaxation, and, yes, that too.

Afterwards, when people used to have the proverbial cigarette, and I was lying with my head in the space between David's shoulder and throat, and he had his arm around my shoulders, I brought up the subject.

'You know when Hoffman said he thought the blackmailing would stop once Sophie was dead?'

'Yes. I know what you're thinking!'

'Well, aren't you too? That must have meant he thought it was Sophie who was blackmailing him.'

'Mmmm. Yeah.'

'So that means it could have been him who killed her to stop her doing that. Now it's going on, he knows it wasn't her.'

'Possibly. It is a motive. I thought so too at the time, or at least when I thought back over what he said. On top of her being a threat to his good name, especially in the States where adultery is looked at more severely. They're a funny lot there. Anyway, I'll definitely follow it up. I'll see he doesn't leave the country until we either clear him or convict him.'

'Does that make him more or less the top of the list now?'

'I don't know. Let me see Sophie's step-dad first. He's due over any day now. Shame. I was rather hoping to have to go back to Barbados!'

I gave his side a gentle thump.

'Without me! Before our holiday? Monster!'

His way of reconciliation was always worth the mock hurts I affected. It went on quite a time. 'Nough said.

Chapter 19

TUESDAY WAS ONE of those days so packed with activities, meetings and deadlines that I forgot to be hungry, and made do with a sandwich eaten at my desk. Half the contents of the paper cup of machine-bought coffee was left to get cold, and then I knocked it over, spoiling several pieces of paper I would have to return to the student whose they were, with an apologetic note scribbled on.

Having missed several days last week only made matters worse. There were piles of papers to read and assess waiting for me on my desk, and kindly colleagues kept arriving to ask how I was and commiserate. Much as I loved my fellow-toilers, I resented the time they took up and the breaks caused in my concentration. I had rather they would take piles of my papers away and deal with them for me as a gift. But I kept my smiling face on as I assured them of my almost complete recovery. After all, if they hadn't come to see me, I would have fretted that I must have hurt or annoyed them in some way, and that would have sapped my energy as well as used up more time.

The afternoon followed the morning's pattern and one of the students for whom I am their personal tutor appeared for a session while I was still deep in writing up the notes for a meeting at which I had been appointed reluctant secretary.

I dismissed him after a few minutes, and felt guilty afterwards. Then I carried on working as colleagues called out their goodbyes as they left for home. Just before seven o'clock I remembered my date with Dr Oakwood and dashed off to the Staff Ladies to check my make-up and hair. All well, although I looked really tired, my forehead scar was itching like mad and the whole front of my head was beginning to throb.

The telephone on my desk rang from the entry security officer to ask if a visitor could be allowed admittance. When Oakwood arrived at my office, I was tidying up the papers on my desk and trying to look as though I was in complete control of my college world.

'Dr Deane? Great to see you. Thanks for agreeing to come out with me tonight.'

'Oh, my pleasure. Nice to meet you.'

We shook hands. I took to him at once. He was as different as could be from Raphael Hoffman. About the same age, roughly mid-40s, but with designer stubble and dressed in 'smart casual'. His thick mop of hair was trendily tousled, what David called the 'just got out of bed' look first made popular forty years ago by Blondie's Debbie Harry.

His look was different from Hoffman's, but his attraction for women would be about the same. It worked for me.

As we made for the street he asked if I minded a walk, of about 10 to 15 minutes. It was what I needed after my day.

'I thought I'd take you to Vanilla Black. OK with you?' Oh, wow. Only my favourite restaurant in the whole of London.

'How did you know I'm a vegetarian?'

'Oh, I've done a little asking around, ' he said enigmatically. 'Actually, I called your husband to ask where he thought you would like to go. His sergeant, nice girl, gave me his card when I (using his fingers to indicate quotation marks) "helped them with their enquiries" a few weeks back. Terrible business that.'

'I'll say. So young, and talented. What a waste.'

'Sure was. I grieve about her every day. I didn't know her that well, but we got along.'

He had known her a bit more that that, I thought.

'I hear you were very generous with her. Bought her lots of expensive presents, that sort of thing.'

'Sure. She was a sweet kid, but loved the good things of life. I liked to make her happy, so bought her stuff. It was a kind of mutual arrangement. She was there for me when I felt a bit lonely sometimes, in a foreign city, far from home and all that. It wasn't like she was underage, or anything. She wasn't my student either. We never met in college. It was her friend, er... Toyah?'

'Yes.'

'It was she who introduced us, and we just sorta hit it off, despite the age difference.

I hit me hard when I heard she'd been killed, and in such a brutal way. Who could do such a thing?'

We walked up Chancery Lane, heads down, thinking our own thoughts, having brought up a subject after which you can hardly engage in idle chat. After a decent while, he broke the silence.

'By the way, call me Gus, will you? And how would you prefer I address you?'

'Julia's fine.'

We turned into a passage which led to Cursitor Street, arrived at Took's Court, and entered the modern, minimalist restaurant. Oakwood was the complete gentleman, and I found I was beginning to enjoy his company more than I had expected.

We studied the menu and laughed together at some of the descriptions. We settled on our choices, offering to share a little of whatever looked interesting on the other's plate. I chose as a starter the Brie icecream and poached blackberries, with quinoa and pickled spring onion; and he, as an avid recent convert to Marmite, took the option of yellow pea soup with Marmite dumplings and sweet onion purée.

While we waited, as well as over that course, we shared brief life stories and got to the point of how we found and admired Dr Charles Burney.

I found Gus's background interesting. Brought up in a bookish family of university teachers in Boston, he first studied and practised law. He even spent some time as an intern on a scholarship at a firm in one of the Inns of Court in London, Middle Temple. Back in the States he quickly rose to become an Assistant

District Attorney in Buffalo, New York, before deciding to switch to the study of music history, which had always been his first love.

'Coming into daily contact with criminals and cops, no offence...'

'None taken.'

'Well, I just thought there was something a bit more life-enhancing than the sordid round of prosecuting the unfortunate – or wicked – whose own lives were usually a mess. Sometimes jail was a relief for them. They could be protected there from the crime gangs that caught them up on every corner.'

With my own recent experience of criminal gangsters, I wanted to move off that subject, so asked what his interest was in the harpsichord, remembering that Toyah had brought him home to show him hers.

'Well, when I was a kid I played piano, as everybody did, at least in my neighbourhood. Then it got kinda samey – everyone trotted out the same old 'Moonlight Sonata', or 'Für Elise'. One day my parents took me to a concert given by Gustav Leonhardt at Harvard, and he not only played harpsichord, brilliantly, but also gave a talk on why period instruments are so important. I was hooked. completely. From that day I just wanted to immerse myself in the music of the past, the period before the Romantics and all that stuff. That's how I got to hear about Burney. That really blew me away when I read about his connections with Handel and Haydn and all those really great guys. What about you?'

I told him, fleetingly, about Helena and Nana Ivy and how I fell in love with Colin Firth's Mr Darcy when I was fifteen, and how I devoured all of Austen and looked for more, for what had inspired her, as nobody comes from nowhere. That's when I found a reference to Fanny Burney in a footnote in *Northanger Abbey*, explaining that Jane Austen greatly admired the author of *Cecilia* and *Camilla*. So I got those books, read the other two Burney novels, and started on her journals and plays.

Then at university I read as much as I could of eighteenth century literature, especially novels by women, and determined to do a Masters in it. That led to the doctorate, and Fanny Burney's father, her siblings, and all their set – Dr Johnson, Sheridan, Reynolds, the lot. I found, and still do, it all totally fascinating.

The next course arrived, just as exotic as the starters. I chose goats' cheese and toasted cauliflower *mille feuille*, with golden raisin and cashew-nut potato and tamarind paste, while Gus enjoyed cornmeal, beetroot and horse radish with black garlic oil and with artichokes in hay, parsley root and hazelnut milk.

How do they think of these things? What fun it must trying out different combinations, and how can veggie food be thought of as dull?

My fork went into a little of Gus's artichoke, while he tried some of my cheese and flaky pastry. He had ordered a bottled of organic Chilean Merlot, which I rather gulped down as an antidote to my frantically busy day.

I asked him, as he poured my second glass, how he had found the now-famous Haydn music manuscript. He chuckled that it was 'all in the book', or would be, when it was published.

'Why were you so keen for young Tom to find out about that?' he asked before finishing off his glass and helping himself to his second.

'Oh, I thought it would help him. He's stuck in the part of his thesis which requires first-hand knowledge of the discovery of original material, and your experience seemed to fit the bill to a tee.'

'Right. That's it?'

'Of course. Which reminds me. Have you seen him recently? I've still heard anything from him.'

'No. No, I haven't. Just the once, several weeks ago, and a phone call fixing up a meeting to which he never showed up. What's going on with that guy? Seems a nice enough fellow. A bit intense, but...'

His voice trailed off, and we finished our dishes in silence.

I began to worry about Tom. It was not like him to ignore my calls and now, not turning up either at Chawton or to see Oakwood, that was weird. Very puzzling.

'Desert?' he enquired as a waiter approached. I declined, and he asked for the bill and settled it without letting me contribute.

The evening was unseasonably mild, and the walk to the Holborn tube station very pleasant. While we passed through Lincoln Inn Fields, Gus recalled some of his more amusing escapades as a young law student in the area.

He left me at the station, and we air-kissed both cheeks in the way that used to be considered Continental, but now was universal.

He was going back down Kingsway to his apartment in Kean Street, his landlord being an old friend from Middle Temple days, now an eminent judge with a couple of properties near the law courts for himself and friends to use when in town, his main residence being the family home in Surrey. It was rather a trek for

Gus to get to the Royal College of Music from there, and would have suited me far better, being very near Kingsway.

Oh well.

I had to change at Kings Cross and caught the next tube to Chalk Farm.

David was home and waiting with an open bottle of wine to greet me after my date.

'How did you get on with Lover-Boy Oakwood? Still consider him a suspect for Sophie's murder?'

'No, not now. There's no point in him killing her. He was quite open about their affair and seemed genuinely fond of her. Anyhow, how about Mac, Sophie's stepdad? Is he here yet?'

'Soon will be. His flight gets in tomorrow, and I'm interviewing him in the afternoon. And your friend Hoffman..'

'Huh! no friend of mine!'

'Well, he came in today with his smartphone and laptop. They've been sent to the technical department but it'll be a few days before he gets them back. He wasn't a bit happy about that, as he's going on tour from tomorrow, different cities across the UK.

Still, he has an agent with him who can do his emailing and texting, but he's such a prima donna. He's been told to report to police stations, one in Edinburgh, one in Leeds and one in Cardiff, and to let me know when he is back in London.

We almost had a row, until his agent pulled him away. Not that he'd ever disturb that immaculate suit of his, but he does like to get his own way, that one.'

We chatted on for a little, said goodnight to Helena, and took the rest of the bottle to the bedroom, drinking as we prepared for bed.

Chapter 20

THE NEXT MORNING I awoke with a thudding headache. Too much wine, and the after effects of the assault still resounding around my skull.

I dragged myself to college and went through the usual routine of meetings, marking, preparing and delivering a lecture, facilitating a seminar and holding tutorials. The rest of the week fitted the same pattern, with the relief of a rehearsal of *The Witlings* and Michael's camp humour to keep me going.

By the weekend I was exhausted. There was one more week to go before going down for the Christmas break. But at least this week entailed no lectures other than the public one I was to give on Musical Performance in the life and work of Fanny Burney.

I had seen the posters and website publicity for this and wondered just how many people in London would be interested, especially as Christmas now seemed so close.

If the weather was bad, or something good was on telly, I imagined the turn-out would be low.

Weeks ago I had suggested that the admin staff responsible for public lectures should contact the Burney Society to advertise it among their members, and was gratified to see some handouts on it at Chawton House when I had gone there.

Now the pressure was on to make it worth it for the punters. I had some time at the weekend, as the whole of the last week was given over to students and their revision, apart from the usual plethora of meetings.

However, I was not prepared for two great shocks on Sunday. One awaited David and me on our return from the 8.30 Mass at the Dominican Priory.

In our living room, where Helena's bed was made up each night and restored to a settee each morning, were Helena and a very smart Mr Hobson from downstairs.

They were holding hands and looking unnaturally sheepish. 'Have a drink', said Helena offering David and me a flute each containing pale bubbling liquid. I saw the open Prosecco bottle on the table behind them.

'What's this about?' asked the great detective.

I guessed, but was astounded.

'Ronald and I are getting married!'

'You? Married?' Not the most gracious thing for a daughter to utter.

Helena, for once, let Ronald do the talking.

'Your mother has done me the honour of accepting my proposal. We've seen a lot of each other these last few weeks, and I don't know anyone who's been able to make me as happy as she has, not since my Evelyn, my first wife, died. Helena's been like a ray of sunshine in my life. Every day with her has been a joy.'

Well, I was speechless. Joy? My mother? And after all the lectures from her about the oppressive institution of marriage. According to her, it had been men's way of ensuring their offspring belong to them and are not somebody else's, so that their work and fortune passes down their own gene line. After not marrying my father and nagging me when I was engaged to David! The cheek!

David took my arm and led me to a chair, putting the glass of bubbly in my hand.

'Well,' he uttered, tentatively. 'Isn't that great! We're pleased for you. Both of us. We really are. Aren't we, Jools?'

'Er....'

'Of course we are, ' he continued. 'Many congratulations. It's just a bit of a shock, that's all. When did this happen? What about the commune? Where will you live?'

Silly question.

'We'll be living right here – downstairs, in Ronald's. It'll be so convenient, especially when you're both really busy, or start a family (throwing a knowing, steely look at me), or something. As for the commune... Well, I wasn't really happy there the last few years, especially when Ann arrived. We didn't really get on. And your father, well, he went off me some time back and I was made to feel a bit out of it, truth to tell. I would have gone back, of course I would, when I'd got my head together. But then I met Ronald and, well, we seem so right for each other. I know I've not been one for marriage before now, but it's what he wants, so that's fine by me too. I just want to make him happy.'

I could see that she did. I could also see that she had been happier, kinder and more considerate recently than I had ever known her. It must have been his influence. Or love (nah!)

More likely the simple fact that someone in this world actually wanted her and cared for her. Well. It was still a shock. A happy shock.

Then I thought of Christmas. Would she be spending it downstairs while Nana Ivy and I, with David's parents, were all whooping it up upstairs? I mentioned the word, and Ronald broke across.

'Oh, don't worry about that for us. I've booked us a lovely cruise over Christmas. We'll have a great time and not bother you at all.'

The mental picture of my mother in her farm-worn jeans and shabby long skirts on a cruise alongside the smart silver surfers made me wince. A shopping trip was called for. Hampstead Bazaar, here we come! Amazingly she consented, and we made plans for the first day I had free after term ended.

We invited them to join us just then for Sunday lunch, after which Ronald expressed his surprise and gratitude than a vegetarian roast meal did not have to be a nut-roast, as he thought that was all we ever lived on.

The food stretched easily to four people as I always cooked more than needed, and often ate the remains up on Monday.

After lunch David and I crashed on the settee in the living room, having finished the sparkling wine and made inroads into a bottle of red.

We snoozed comfortably, his arm round my shoulders, my head on his. Suddenly we were jolted awake by the ringing tone, a real brrrrrring-brrrrrrring, on the mobile David only used for work. Something important.

Must be.

It was.

It was the second shock of the day, and a complete contrast to the first. A body had been found, that of a young man. It had been discovered in a shallow grave in Epping Forest, and the Essex police thought it might be of interest to the Met. The cause of death resembled that of Sophie's. A stabbing, then throttling. The face was so beaten up that not even dental records could be of much use. A post-mortem would be held first thing on Monday morning, and DNA samples were already being sent to the lab for analysis at the same time.

David's team had urged the Essex police to make it a top priority. Otherwise the wait for results could take days or weeks.

David came off the phone and reported what he had been told. I just felt a huge surge of sorrow. Another young life cut short. Another grieving family and bewildered friends.

'It might have nothing to do with Sophie, even if the MO is the same,' David conjectured. 'This body was buried. Sophie's wasn't. This one is in Epping, Sophie's in Hampstead. Two very different scenes. There could be a thousand reasons for this one – gang related, whatever.'

The warm glow of a winter's Sunday afternoon after a good meal had quickly turned icy. We got up off the settee and I went to unpack the dishwasher and then do some work on my public lecture, while David started a round of phone calls to colleagues, taking notes while he did so.

I almost dropped one of our good dinner plates with a sudden hideous thought. I went to the living room and waved to David to stop talking and to listen to me.

'Just a minute, I'll call you back. Julia's got something she wants me for. Well?', looking up at me.

'I know this could be a long shot. But what if it's Tom!' 'Tom?'

'Yes, you know – the postgrad I was going to take with me to Chawton when I thought I was going. The young man I've been trying to reach and who never got back to me.'

David did not dismiss the idea, and took down all the details I could remember of Tom. I looked up his phone number from my diary and gave it to him.

I went back to my domestic chore and could hear David passing on Tom's details to his team. Thinking of Tom lying in the woods with his face a bloody mess, his last minutes on earth totally terrifying for him, drew my tears. I began to shiver.

I went back and sat besides David once more, drawing close to feel the comfort of his warm, solid body, while he continued his calls, holding the phone in his right hand and putting his left arm around me.

Why on earth should anyone want to kill Tom? Unless he was the blackmailer. Nonsense. He couldn't be. Could he? Did he know the same people? He didn't even go to the same college as Sophie. Had he even heard of Hoffman, other than as a famous pianist, and probably not at all of Smith-Humphries – a little-known local piano teacher living in Norfolk? Hardly....surely?

No, he was not the blackmailing sort. Far too anxious and self-doubtful.

Anyway, it was too early to speculate. He could be any young man – probably a local Essex or East End drug dealer who had tried to swindle a customer, or something. No point in dwelling on it.

So, I got up and went into the kitchen where I spread my papers out and got on with work.

On Monday morning David gave me a lift to Chalk Farm station on his way to his cop shop. I spent the day with a series of students, individually and in groups.

At lunchtime I went to the refectory with a few close colleagues. We talked mainly about exams, and which students had special needs for which specific arrangements had to be made. More student meetings in the afternoon while I anxiously awaited news from David. Nothing all day.

I got back home at about 6.30 and was met at the front door by Helena, keen to show me round Ronald's flat. I had been in there before, but there had been changes, mainly in the arrangement of furniture and some new replacement items. She had certainly brightened it up.

Gone was the mustiness and clutter, old ornaments and piles of papers. There were new curtains and cushions, bed covers and tablecloths. I had to admit it was a great improvement. She beamed at my congratulations at the transformation, and offered to make us a cup of tea. I was in a hurry to get home so suggested that next time would be good, but was touched by her consideration.

David came in shortly after me, took off his coat and shoes, then came and hugged me. I realised what this meant.

'It is your Tom, ' he confirmed. 'I am so sorry.'

When I finished weeping, we had a scrappy meal of bread, cheese and the rest of the red wine. He told me that I might be needed for questioning, obviously not by him, but to fill in some of the facts of that young, and private, man.

It seemed Tom had few friends, and none close, being too serious and studious to develop a social life. His parents were estranged, and there were no contact details for either of them in his rooms. However, they would be tracked down, as would the killer.

Meanwhile, David urged me to give it no more thought, but to concentrate on next day's public lecture. He would have loved to have come, but would now be far too busy on this new case.

That was fine with me, as I was always highly nervous when speaking in public with him in the audience. Strangers were fine. Afterward the talk I would bore him with it all, or at least that's what I had done in the past. This time something more significant would take place after my talk to worry about repeating it to him.

Chapter 21

TUESDAY EVENING, SIX o'clock. I stood before a reasonably full lecture hall in the Strand campus and delivered my talk, making a few jokes that always warmed an audience up and helped me to relax and ad lib. Among the dark anoraks and quilted jackets worn by most in the hall, I noticed a more groomed and better dressed listener. Oh, God, It's Hoffman! What's he doing here?

Applause.

Questions from the floor, which I fielded fairly well, I thought. There is usually at least one individual who knows more about some detail or other than does the lecturer, and who seems to have a mission in life to score one over the hapless speaker. There was one of those tonight. If the Burneys were still alive, he would have known them personally. He asked his lengthy and erudite question, which lost me somewhere along the line. I tried to summarize the point he was making in order to answer it, and somehow made him and the audience believe I knew of what I was talking. Not strictly true, but let that pass.

After that I scanned the hall, but Hoffman had gone. A group of enthusiasts clustered around the lectern and bombarded me with questions, some of which were interesting. I answered those I could, and to the others I had to rummage in my brain to find something to satisfy them.

I was introduced by one of the audience to two or three others. To be honest, I wasn't taking it in, disturbed at the earlier sight of Raphael Hoffman. Seeing him made me feel a weakness around my knees, and caused me to breathe in short bursts. I had to get a grip over myself.

Eventually I was rescued by Anne-Marie, a colleague from the department who had kindly supported me by attending the talk. We collected our coats and left.

Outside was cold and dark, but still bustling with late commuters or excited theatre-goers. We walked together up Kingsway, from where Anne-Marie caught her bus home. I went into the George Eliot building and greeted Martin, the security officer in his open office just inside the doorway. After that I took the lift to the sixth floor, showed my security card to the scanner on the two sets of doors leading to the corridor on which is my office, and walked along to it.

As with all the offices in the modern building the college recently took over, I have a bright and airy room with a computer desk on which is an Anglepoise lamp, and there are three padded chairs surrounding a small round table for interviews or tutorials. A filing cabinet and book shelving completes the fittings and fixtures.

I could see well enough from the corridor lighting not to bother to switch on the lights. I dumped my folder of notes and flash-stick of the lecture on the desk, picked up a scarf from the back of my chair, and turned to the door. Woops! My memory.

I went back to the desk, opened a drawer and picked up a sheaf of notes paper-clipped together which I would read on the Tube going home. My face was turned away from the door, when the poor light suddenly dimmed even further. A tall figure was blocking the doorway. I turned and peered, but could barely make out his features against the corridor light behind him. When he spoke I knew. Hoffman. My stomach lurched.

'Dr Deane!'

I spluttered out, 'How did you get in? What do you want?'

'It's easy enough. The guy at the desk was distracted so I slipped by, and a couple of students kindly let me pass through the security doors.'

He took a step into the room. I took a step back. He raised his arm to show me a newspaper half unfolded in his hand.

'What I want, Dr Deane, is for your husband to stop this witch-hunt.'

I had the presence of mind to reach to the lamp switch on the desk to prevent his having the advantage of seeing me while he remained a featureless form. He thrust the paper towards me.

'Do you see this?' he menaced, shaking the paper.

'No, I've not seen the paper today. I've been too busy.'

'Well look at it! See?'

I saw a headline: 'Another student murdered'.

Oh my God – I felt entitled to use that near-blasphemous cliche, although silently. He's involved in that!

'See?' He read out, 'Hoffman in trouble with the police'.

Oh, that headline. Next to the one about the murdered student. This one had a picture of Hoffman arriving at a police station.

'First your friend blackmails me, I'm sure of it. Then your policeman husband goes back on his word to keep me out of the papers! When are you going to be through with me? Well?'

By now he was shouting, almost shaking with anger. I felt real alarm and could not get the words together in my mind that would extricate me. Suddenly another person arrived, as tall and well built as the raging Hoffman.

'Say, is this man troubling you, Julia?'

Thank God. It was Gus, Gus Oakwood. Another American, this time a friendly one. He took control immediately.

'Hey, you're Raphael Hoffman, aren't you? I noticed you earlier, at the lecture. You've no right to threaten Dr Deane like that. Get outta here. Calm down!'

Hoffman seemed suddenly deflated. He took some noisy deep breaths and scowled at Oakwood. Then he turned away.

'You're welcome to her, ' he growled. 'Damn you and damn her.'

He made off along the corridor and away. Gus came towards me.

'I thought I might find you here. I wanted to see you after the talk. Say, that was really good, by the way. What did that guy want with you? You know who he is, I guess? He didn't sound too friendly. '

I let out a laugh at that understatement, and began to relax.

'I'm so glad you're here. That was horrible. Y'know, I still feel a bit fragile. Actually....'

I began to cry, real weepy tears. Although I am always speaking in public and have been doing so for years, I never the less approach each occasion with a nervousness that tenses me up. Plus I had not slept well. Tears, which I would normally despise in a woman, were now a natural release.

In seconds, Gus had his arms round me, pressing me to him as I sobbed against his chest. Then I pulled away gently, put down the papers I had been holding back onto the desk – no reading tonight – and turned out the lamp.

'Come round to mine. You could do with a stiff drink. And then I'll run you home. My car is parked real near my place.'

It was an offer I had no wish to refuse.

It was but a very short walk to his apartment in Kean Street, just off Drury Lane. Tucked between a prestigious office complex and the back of the Delaunay Restaurant, it was a smart modern first floor flat right in the heart of theatre land.

The bracing December air helped to restore my vigour and I enjoyed Gus's jokey comments. He showed me briefly round the apartment and invited me to sit on one of the surprisingly – or perhaps, fashionably – shabby armchairs in the living room while he went into the kitchen to pour the drinks.

'Scotch?' he asked from the unseen room.

'Please, with a little water.'

He called, 'Ice?'

'No thanks.'

While he was fixing the drinks I took the Oyster card from my coat pocket to put in my handbag, as I would not be needing it with the proffered lift. I lost the grip and it slipped from my cold fingers and slid down the side of the chair cushion. That is always so annoying. I pushed my hand down between the seat cushion and the armrest, fingertipped the card, and felt another object down there, something paper. I drew out both items and opened my bag, unzipping the inner pocket, and popped in my Oyster travel card.

Then I looked quickly at the nature of the folded piece of paper, partly from naughty curiosity and partly to see if it was something important, the finding of which would please my host. I just folded back the top third to read the email details:

From: no-reply@edreams.com
Subject: Booking confirmation LFT27T39PL28
Date: 26 November 2014 14.50
To: Tom Jacobs tomjacobs1994@aol.com

Tom! My God, no. Tom! I quickly opened out and scanned the rest of the paper. Nearly halfway down it said again, in larger print: Booking Confirmation, and below it, a tick and white letters against a dark blue background, 'This is the e-ticket for your booking', and lower down listed details included the words 'Vienna'.

What was Tom's airline ticket doing here? My mind raced and with adrenalin pumping fast round my body, my immediate thought was David.

I plunged my hand into my bag and drew out my mobile, stabbing at the speed dial. After what seemed like an age, though must have been only a second or two, and while I heard the sound of clinking glasses approaching, I just managed to whisper-shout

'David', when a hand reached down and prized the phone from my grasp. I looked up at Gus Oakwood, glaring at me, and then at the paper in my hand.

Chapter 22

'WHAT ARE YOU DOING with Tom's travel ticket?'

Then I asked without thinking. 'Did you kill him?'

Oakwood calmly put down the drinks tray and opened up my phone. Deftly he removed the SIM card and dropped it into his trouser pocket.

'You don't have to involve your husband in everything, you know. And I don't know why you're bothered about that little blackmailing prick. Unless you set him up?'

My long-term prospects suddenly looked far from good. Every nerve in my body was now on full alert.

He turned and withdrew into the kitchen while I made a dash for the door, heart thumping.

I turned briefly to see him return almost immediately with a knife in his hand. But I had opened the door and slammed it shut behind me.

By the time he was through it I was flying down the stairs, literally taking several at a time. I made it through the inner hall door then sped on through the front door and was out into the street, running for my life.

He was close behind, but I was sprinting like an Olympian. Two people were walking towards us on Drury Lane and it passed through my mind to stop them and ask for their assistance, but reckoned the delay in explaining could be fatal and he would then be on to me.

The middle aged couple looked startled as I sped towards them with a man in pursuit.

Oakwood then had the presence of mind to call out 'Darling! Come back! We can sort this out!' – making it seem like a marital tiff, not a death race.

I passed them and hurried on, making for Aldwich and crowds of people, even possibly, police officers.

My running was impressive, but his was faster. Just outside the Aldwich Theatre, he caught my upper arm and yanked me to a stop. My shoulder would have hurt had I not been numb with fear. Wordlessly, but with the knife glinting near my throat, he held onto my arm and forced me with him back in the direction of his flat.

There was no-one around to witness this abduction. A few minutes earlier the place would have been thronged. Just my luck.

We were walking in the roadway, and as we reached the entrance of the apartment building, instead of entering, he pulled me towards a short row of cars parked opposite to it on residents permits. Passing two or three cars, we reached his. He opened the driver's door, and pushed me hard into the seat, indicating for me to clamber over the gearstick console into the passenger's side.

With his knife flashing, I simply did as he directed, and clambered into the passenger's seat. He followed me in and told me, with apparent solicitude, to strap myself in. I suppose he did not want us to be stopped for a minor infringement when he had murder in mind.

He started the car, and I realized his slight delay in following me from the kitchen could have been in collecting the knife or his car keys from wherever he kept them.

He drove, looking intently ahead, with his eyes narrowed in anger. I had not thought the amiable Gus capable of such a hard expression, nor of such bloody deeds.

I tried to notice where we were going. We were crossing Waterloo Bridge, and I spotted a set of CCTV cameras half way across. I bent as far forward as I could as I wanted the cameras to make out my face.

Several times I tried mouthing 'help' to passers-by when we slowed or stopped at lights or crossings, but nobody noticed, or they thought I was drunk.

Oakwood had applied the child lock, so I could not open the door to escape, though I tried. We spoke not a word. I realized it is only in films that the killer goes to great length to explain his crimes before ending the life of his victim. In reality, why should he?

At one point, stopping at lights, he electronically opened his window, took something from his jacket pocket and jettisoned it through the window. From the tiny tinkle as it hit the ground, I assumed it was my SIM card. No chance of tracing my movements now. My despair hit new depths.

He drove on, his eyes looking resolutely forward, never at me. I wondered if he knew where he was going, or was just keeping on the move.

We passed a stationery police car and I turned to gesticulate to them.

'Sit straight. Don't move. Look forward,' he ordered gruffly.

I could not tell what was going on in his mind. He gave nothing away.

We stopped at lights at a major junction, and could hear the siren of a police car behind us. It could have been the same one we had just passed. This one was approaching at speed and overtaking the row of cars behind us. It did not want seem to be slowing for the lights, although they were still on red.

Suddenly, seemingly on impulse, Oakwood swung the wheel to the right and slammed his foot on the accelerator. Just at that moment the police car, with a squeal of brakes, ploughed broadside into our car, the driver's side taking the full impact.

There was the expected bang and crunching sound. Then silence, broken only by tinkling glass and a low moan from Oakwood. I was clearly aware that my right arm was squashed and trapped by Oakwood's body and that I had no breath left in my lungs. After the fraction of a second, I began to feel excruciating pain and shock. Then merciful darkness.

Chapter 23

I CAME TO BLEARY consciousness in an ambulance, hearing the woo-woo siren right above me, and feeling my hand being enfolded in that of a young, gentle, black paramedic.

'Hi, there!' he greeted me, as from another planet. 'Good to see you! Can you tell me your name?'

'Julia'

'Hi, Julia.'

'How is he? The driver?' Why I was keen to know I cannot imagine.

'I'm sorry', he said, like he really meant it. 'He is really badly hurt. Who is he, your husband?'

'God, no. He was going to murder me. He already killed two people.'

'Yeah?' – as in, humour her, she's in shock.

Talking nonsense is part of it.
I didn't bother.

*　　　　*　　　　*

David's face appeared with increasing clarity. He was watching mine intently as I emerged into full consciousness. The white mist in which I had been floating gradually took on the solid shapes and forms of a hospital room. David's voice, previously heard as mumbled sound through thick cotton wool, was gently forming words. No sight was more welcome to me than that of his face, nor no sound more precious. I realised that he was all I had ever wanted or needed. Romantic heroes? Forget them. David – good, dependable, hardworking, faithful David. Who could be a better man to wake up to, either in hospital or in bed?

'Oh, Jools. Darling. It's so good to have you back. You really had me worried for a time. But everything's all right. You're going to be fine. The arm and ribs will heal up, and no serious damage done. Your head took a knock, you must have bashed it on the head-rest or on Oakwood's head. That made the previous bang those bastards gave you cause the blackout.

You're up to your eyes in painkillers too, so don't worry if you can't think straight.'

He was babbling with relief.

'Love you,' I managed.

'Oh, I love you too. My God, I do!'

'Tell me everything,' I asked, with eyes closing against the glare of daylight. 'How long have I been out?'

'About eighteen hours, love. And a lot's been going on while you've been snoozing!'

'What, tell me. I was in a car....with Gus.....what happened? Is he all right?'

I was more interested in the criminal enquiry.

David patiently explained all the loose ends, more than once as I could not take everything in the first time.

When Tom's body had been found, Sophie's boyfriend, Mark Brizzi, had walked into the police station and given himself up. He and Sophie had been behind the blackmailing; he using his advanced computer skills that impressed even his tutors at Imperial College. He had also used college devices and a series of cheap pay-as-you-go telephones, registered in false names, to avoid detection.

When Smith-Humphries had failed to pay up in cash all the money demanded, he and Sophie had been the ones to post the hateful messages, driving him to his death.

He and Sophie had also been blackmailing Hoffman, knowing the affair could ruin his reputation. Brizzi had continued to do so even after Sophie's death.

Blackmailing Oakwood came about when Brizzi had hacked into Oakwood's private electronic correspondence and found that the much-vaunted discovery of the Haydn manuscript, the letters to Burney and all of that, had been a brilliant act of forgery.

The actual perpetrators were underground experts Oakwood had encountered from his days prosecuting criminals. He had commissioned them to produce authentic-seeming paper, ink and to write in the eighteenth-century manner at his dictation. The music itself was all Oakwood's, the product of years of studying Haydn's musical style under the tutelage of H.C. Robins Landon.

The schloss in Austria was owned by a friend and collaborator, who was prepared to pretend to have had the masterpiece hidden away in an obscure folder in his library.

The crime itself would have enabled Oakwood to make his name and fortune. Before Oakwood died he told the police that he had realized that Sophie had known of the forgery and was his blackmailer, so she had to die. Her coat and his and the murder weapons were all jettisoned into a lake, weighted down. The cello and its case were too bulky to dispose of in that way and could float. So they were buried in Epping Forest, not far from where Tom's body was found.

'But Tom?'

It seems that Tom had got too close to discovering the truth of the discovery of the manuscript, and by going to Austria to investigate, could have uncovered more than Oakwood had been prepared for. Oakwood believed that he might have got it wrong about Sophie, and began to think that Tom himself could have been the blackmailer. One way or the other, Tom had to go too.

Poor Tom. I had pushed him into that. Guilt descended like a shroud. David held onto both my hands and was just telling me not be silly thinking like that when a surprise visitor appeared.

Nana Ivy.

'So, my darling. What's all this then? What's been happening in my Julia's world?'

Where to start?

Proof

Made in the USA
Charleston, SC
05 June 2015